CENTER
OF THE WORLD

▲

CENTER OF THE WORLD

▲

Native American Spirituality

As told by
Plains Cree Pipe Keeper
Don Rutledge
with
Rita Robinson

Newcastle Publishing Co., Inc.
North Hollywood, California
1992

Edited by Nancy Shaw Strohecker & James Stuart Strohecker
Cover Design by Michele Lanci-Altomare
Illustrations by Barbara Cunningham

This book is not intended to diagnose, prescribe, or treat any ailment, nor is it intended in any way as a replacement for medical con-
sultation when needed. The author and publishers of this book do
not guarantee the efficacy of any of the methods herein described,
and strongly suggest that at the first sign of any disease or disorder
the reader consult a physician.

FIRST EDITION
A NEWCASTLE BOOK
First printing, 1992
10 9 8 7 6 5 4 3 2 1
Printed in the United States of America

For my mother,
Alta Lee

OTHER BOOKS BY RITA ROBINSON

▲

The Friendship Book

When Women Choose to be Single

When Your Parents Need You

Survivors of Suicide

The Palm

ACKNOWLEDGMENTS

▲

The authors would like to thank the following people for helping make the book possible:

Joe Iron Man
Aunt Jenny Gray
Loren Nelson
C. B. Clark
Dennis Zotigh
Mae Velasquez
Fran Dancing Feather
Dean Allen
Jenny Busby
Leonard and Beulah Wheatley
Barbara Cunningham
Jessica Licona
Nancy Shaw Strohecker

CONTENTS

▲

ILLUSTRATIONS

▲

PREFACE

▲

The Native American can never return to the buffalo hunt, but we can have our heritage wherever we are. This spirituality enriches the lives of people who hunger today for a more balanced world in which we are in harmony with nature.

At one time, all the Native American people were in touch with the universe and the sacred circle, including Mother Earth, Father Sun, the moon, the rain, thunder and lightning. We were aware of the seasons because they touched our naked bodies and spirit.

We believe that all living things, including the four-legged, the winged, the finned, the crawling animals, the trees, rocks, rivers, oceans, as well as man and woman are made by the Creator. We share space with these things. We do not dominate or conquer them.

We live in one of the most technologically advanced nations in the world. Yet, we are deprived of our ties to the earth, the wind, the air, the rain, the thunder, the animals . . . our roots and our spirituality.

Mother Teresa, the Catholic Nun who works with the world's poorest, once said during a visit to the United States that American faces are the most blank and unhappy of any she had ever witnessed. Well-known actor and comedian, Robin Williams, who is also an activist, once said during an interview that America may have everything but a soul.

According to Native Americans, however, the spirit or soul is not so easy to kill because it is all around us. We are the center of all that is happening. Each individual is the center of the world. Where you stand is the center of the universe. All else surrounds you. But most importantly, in our circle we are one with the universe and dependent on everything we touch, see, smell, taste, hear, feel, sense, and experience. With this understanding comes a great sense of responsibility and awe.

Native American spirituality is that simple. At the same time, however, it appears complex because so many conflicting traditions seem to exist throughout the different tribes. Even though Native Americans have appeared in gatherings to have closed minds about other ceremonies, beliefs and paths, all tribes and traditions are connected and in the same circle. Each tribe has a valid reason for doing ceremony according to their traditions because of sacred visions experienced by their own medicine people.

The condition of the earth today brings great pain and tears to the Native American, and uncertainty for the unborn children of the world. I believe that the only way we can begin to heal Mother Earth is by taking personal responsibility for our own circle. We can begin by understanding a little of what is happening to our earth, and how some technology is destroying, not saving, us. I believe, like many Native Americans, that we need a rebirth of our spiritual heritage to heal ourselves and our planet.

The National Wildlife Federation offers some interesting observations about how technology is dealing with our environmental problems:

▲ In 1970, the official U.S. endangered species list contained 92 names. Today, that number is over 500.
▲ Estimated global pesticide sales in 1975 were $5 billion. Today they have reached $50 billion.
▲ Billions of board feet of timber harvested from U.S. Forest Service lands in 1970 was 11.5. In 1988, 12.6.

▲ One hundred million tons of solid waste was generated by Americans in 1970. It's well above 150 million today.

On the positive side, the number of wildlife refuges has increased from 331 in 1970 to 452 in 1989. Miles of designated U.S. Wild and Scenic Rivers in 1970 was 868. By 1989, it was 9,278.

Our technology is also developing solar and electric-powered automobiles, and business is now touting more environmentally sound products.

These developments are to be commended, but it is still the spirit that is yet to be dealt with. I believe that we must be able to "feel" and have compassion for our environment, this Mother Earth, or all the technology in the world won't save us.

To most Native Americans, living in harmony with his or her environment is paramount to life and existence. The development of an electric teakettle that breaks down into recyclable parts, or switching to unbleached coffee filters does not provide the answers we need to live in balance and harmony with the earth and sky. "Things" do not give us spirit. Interconnectedness, spirituality, honor, and reverence provide our means for wholeness.

Demolish a river or a forest with acid rain and a part of us is destroyed. Fill the sky with pollutants and we both offend Father Sky and kill a bit of ourselves. Yet, we realize and cherish the renewed concern by environmentalists to help restore our Mother Earth. We are heartened by the drives for more recycling, cleaner water, protection of our forests, and havens for endangered species. We praise energy conservation movements and the growing concern for other cultures.

Native Americans try to follow the "Red Path," which flows with nature. We are connected in the same way to all things of creation. We're aware, though, that in addition to the Red Path, there is also the "Black" one which goes against the flow.

Red is the positive way. Black is the negative. Both are necessary, but our goal is to keep to the Red Path and pay attention
to the lessons we can learn from the Black, or negative world.

Technological societies often stray into Black Paths, but we
will not always have the choice of returning to the Red Path
after the death of the world's delicate balance.

Native Americans are not calling for a "return to nature."
Rather, we feel we must embrace what is left of creation and
try to heal—make good medicine—within our lives in the ce-
ment cities we have constructed. Our cities, after all, are built
on and of the earth. Our food, though tainted with chemicals
and pollutants, still requires nurturing from the earth, rain,
and sun. Our very lives are entwined with every other life
form, be it a stone or a river. All of these things have life force
or "spirit." As Carl Sagan said, "We are the stuff of stars." So
is everything else in creation.

Our beliefs, our rituals, our ceremonies, our pain and our
suffering, are not a religion; they are a way of life. In that way,
all of the nearly two million Native Americans living in the
United States (from the eight major language families) are
united as one. We are connected to all races: black, yellow, and
white, in the same way that we are connected to the oceans,
the animals and the earth.

When John Donne, the 16th century English poet wrote,
"No man is an island, entire of itself; every man is a piece of
the continent, a part of the main. . . ," he tapped into a feeling of oneness with the universe. He also wrote, "Man is but
earth; 'Tis true; but earth is the centre."

Today people are in search of a greater awareness of our ties
to the earth, sky, and other humans. What I offer here is but
one way—a path, and this path like all others leads to the
center of the circle.

Following my path has not been easy and I have strayed
many times. Yet, the Creator ultimately guides me back. Since

I do not look Indian, many Native Americans do not initially accept me as a pipe keeper. Also, because my pipe-keeping ceremonies are for helping people who live in cities rather than on the reservation, it's more difficult for me to find the needed balance. On the reservation, one is able to feel secure and in tune with creation. In the city, one is subject to so many negative pulls and influences, as well as seeing and feeling the pollution of unclear skies.

I have undertaken this book because it is my path to help educate people in what I believe is a correct Native American way, and to show the richness and the true spirit of our culture.

Earth's Shadows

Oh Great Mother, your face is changing.
You're getting older.
Nuclear sadness in your belly brings pain.
Sky is brown above your head,
And your Native children cry.

But the great bird shall break free one day.
He will shake the earth,
Crumbling the great towers to the dusty ground,
Laying waste to the greedy lovers of power,
Putting things back the way they used to be.

Oh Great Mountain, I'm getting older too.
My voice is cracking, when I'm defending you.
My song is out of tune.
The way of my people is dying,
Replaced by ignorance and war.

From the top of the Sacred Mountain,
To the crashing waves of your great oceans,

The simple truth remains.
Poisoned waters flow from the Continental Divide,
To the edges of the land of your dark children.

All that is left are the artifacts,
The handmade jewelry and loom-woven blankets.
The ruins of the ancients are trampled by the curious,
And the drunken "Indian" stumbles in the streets. . . .

But somewhere the Rainbow Warrior sails.
The "Earth First" children sit in patient protest
Among the redwood forests, never giving in.
The people say consciousness is raising.
Patience! Patience! Faith must long endure.

There are lodges, deep within the shadowed forests,
Where the old ones enter the dreams of the children,
Saying "Dry your eyes, for we will live free again
Where the wild cougar walks in peace
And the eagle soars in unpolluted visions
And Grandmother river sings to the seekers of peace."

Fran Dancing Feather
Big Bear City, Calif.

NATIVE AMERICAN HERITAGE

▲

I am French and Plains Cree on my mother's side. On father's side, I am Scottish and Dutch. My Native American heritage traces back to my mother's Cree ancestors in Canada who took part in the Louis Riel rebellion in 1885.

The Canadians, like the Americans, were also conquerors. But when they tried to take Cree and Metis hunting lands, a rebellion broke out. Metis (May-tee) are Plains Cree half-bloods—part French, Dutch, or Scottish.

The rebellion was unsuccessful, and bands of displaced Cree and Metis sought political asylum in the United States. They were not able to resettle in the United States until 1905, however. At that point, they got a reservation known as Rocky Boy's Agency in North, central Montana near the Bear Paw Mountains. My mother's people didn't stop in Montana, but instead fled to Oklahoma where they started new lives and blended in. Other rebellious bands of Cree and Metis, fearing reprisal from the Canadian government, moved to different parts of the United States.

The Cree originally lived around the Great Lakes of Canada. The smallpox epidemic of the late 1700s and early 1800s, nearly destroyed the Cree in Canada. They scattered and lived meagerly by hunting and trapping. Many of the remaining Plains Cree took on the ways of other tribes they contacted. The other tribes also took some of the Cree's traditions and rituals. As a result, the merging of many traditions took place.

This merging of traditions continued after the exodus from Canada following the Louis Riel rebellion, with the Crees blending with the Chippewa, Ojibwa, Soto, Sioux, Blackfoot, and Assiboines Indians, along with the French and Scottish. Today Cree bands live in Canada, Saskatchewan, Manitoba, Ontario, Quebec, as well as North Dakota and Montana, according to Adolph Hungry Wolf's introduction to *My Cree People*, by Fine Day.

I did not grow up on a reservation, nor did I learn of my heritage until my late thirties. At that time, I was told that my grandfather on my mother's side, whose name I carried, was actually my step-grandfather. My real grandfather, Will Wilson, was a full-blood Plains Cree. To this day, I have never been able to find out if he was from Oklahoma or Canada. My grandmother had kept my heritage a secret in order to give me the benefits of growing up white, instead of the heartaches of a Native American. My grandmother's thoughts were, "After all, who wanted to be an Indian?"

My Metis grandmother, my mother's mother, from Oklahoma, did not look Native American. Most of her life she wanted to be white, and she did so very successfully. My mother, however, did look Native American, especially with her beautiful dark hair and skin. At various times, I overheard different comments as a child about my mother being Indian. My grandmother ignored me when I mentioned it, or asked questions about it. My mother only smiled, knowing she was forbidden to acknowledge her heritage in front of her mother. We were also not allowed to use the word "Indian" around my grandmother.

Still, my mother recalls being called "nigger," "gut eater," and "blanket ass" by the white kids. They knew her origins by her appearance. They threw rocks at her and her cousins on the way home from school.

My grandmother wanted to protect me from this racism. That's why the secret of my real grandfather, her first husband and the father of my mother, remained a secret until just before she died. At that time, my mother told me the story of my Cree and Metis blood.

With this knowledge, I attended Native American studies classes at California State University at Long Beach in 1979 and 1980. I started then what has become a vast Native American library and did so much reading that I had to get glasses.

At about the same time, I began doing volunteer work in Los Angeles at various Native American centers. My work involved the Indian Child Welfare Act of 1978, which was designed to keep Native American children in the homes of Native Americans. I also helped in Native American community development, and in EONA (Educational Opportunities for Native Americans) Title IV, involving Native American education.

Although I was studying my culture, working in the Indian community and attending powwows, I still had yet to discover my true spiritual path.

Like many other Native Americans, my life's path was not clear. My spirituality evolved slowly after I had spent my teen years in Long Beach working in the oil fields as a welder's apprentice for my father's business. I started at the age of eleven and spent every summer vacation, holiday and weekend working. A month after I turned seventeen, I joined the Air Force to get away from that hard life. Eventually, I transferred to the Strategic Air Command.

After serving in the military, I went back into the oil field welding business as the youngest journeyman welder there. I also rode with many outlaw motorcyclists in Southern California at this time. Although I never got involved with drugs I had recurring bouts with alcohol. Over the years I also worked as a bodyguard, truck driver, fumigation chemist, and private investigator before returning to work for the same oil field welding company for fifteen years in sales and management.

During this time I fathered three children, one during a marriage. Following a divorce, I fought for custody of my five-year-old son and raised him for thirteen years until he entered college.

In some ways my path is not unlike that of other Native Americans who eventually find their way back to their spiritual heritage and try to follow the teachings of their ancestors. For many of us, the return is a struggle for the rest of our lives.

I was led to an Indian reservation and received a vision which revealed my life's path. Most Native American medicine people receive visions that guide them on their separate and unique paths. We all travel through life uncovering what is necessary for our existence. Some do it through visions, and many, like myself never reveal their personal visions to anyone. I have found that it is only when we ignore our path that we lose sight of our way, and our lives become meaningless.

In 1985, I received my first "vision" and unexpectedly became a medicine person. This happened at a place near a small group of mountains nicknamed the Little Rockies, on the Fort Belknap reservation in Montana. I originally went there to receive a healing from a medicine man for my son who had been injured in an automobile accident. I also wanted to get my pipe purified so I could use it as a family prayer pipe. I wanted to do some Native American research too, at the Rocky Boy's Indian Reservation about eighty miles west of Belknap. This reservation was founded by Stone Child (Rocky Boy) for the Chippewa and Cree.

Many unexpected things occurred during the trip that I did not fully understand until much later. In retrospect, I'm sometimes still in awe of what did happen. I know now that the Creator, the grandfathers, and the thunderbird chose my path and made me a pipe keeper.

The thunderbird in most traditions is a supernatural being,

often a raven or other animal that takes on human form. In *The World of the American Indian*, John C. Ewers, former curator of the Museum of the Plains Indians, says that the Plains Indians dreaded the thunder. They visualized the thunderbird as a giant bird carrying an arrow in its talons, ready to hurl it earthward as lightening. They believed such power could kill a man.

My thoughts on the thunderbird are about the same, except I don't believe it takes on human or raven form. I feel that the thunderbird blindly flies in and out of thunder heads, and lightening flashes forth when the thunderbird opens its eyes. On a stormy night with thunder and lightening, it might be possible to see the thunderbird. Whenever the thunderbird comes down it is terrifying, and it often brings destruction through the lightening from its eyes. I call it a "cleansing," and when it's over, it reminds me of the calm and purification after a storm.

I have no idea why I was chosen for the sacred pipe ceremony, and am still moved by the entire experience which I feel was a test. The thunderbird has its reasons when it tests us. I believe it is to see if one is worthy of the path chosen by the Creator.

During this time at the reservation I stayed with an elder, Aunt Jenny. She was a small, round, simply dressed, and humble medicine woman. Disabled from birth, she walked with a limp. Although her eyes were failing with age, they still sparkled. Her energy permeated the area when I was around her.

Across the road from her prefab house was the old one-room log cabin where she and her husband lived before his death. They used to ride horseback together when her husband went hunting for meat in the beginning of their marriage in the early 1900s. Aunt Jenny had no children but raised about fourteen belonging to her extended family.

Aunt Jenny was highly regarded for her medicine ways. I

learned a great deal from her, not only through her words, but from watching her. She also watched me from the corner of her eye.

During the two weeks on the reservations, we stayed up late in the evenings drinking coffee and talking about the old medicine ways. When she began talking, she would always say, ''I shouldn't be telling you this, but I want you to hear it the right way.'' Then she would proceed with her medicine talk.

FIRST CEREMONY

At the reservation, Joe Iron Man, a full-blooded Plains Cree and Holy Man who lived with his wife at Fort Belknap, was ready to do the ceremony to purify my sacred pipe and do the healing for my son.

The ceremony included healings for several other Native Americans and lasted until early morning. Eventually the healing came around the circle to me. I was engulfed in a vision where time stood still and the outside world didn't exist. I lost awareness of all others in the circle except for the Holy Man and Aunt Jenny. Their presence comforted and made me feel protected. Although I was confused and didn't understand what was happening at the time, I felt very calm afterwards. When the ceremony was over, Joe Iron Man told me that he would explain my vision and I would need to be purified in the sweat lodge. He also said that the Creator and the grandfathers had instructed him to show me pipe directions. I didn't understand what this meant and that my experience had brought me into the realm of medicine people.

Joe told me he had to cut wood early the next morning for the sweat in the afternoon. I asked if he needed some help. He seemed surprised and replied, ''That's a change. About the only time I usually see anyone is after I've cut the wood, and have started the fire to heat the rocks. They see the smoke and then they come."

Early in the morning, we went into the woods to collect and cut deadfall trees. It was so thick that we had to weave in and out through the forest. The same types of trees had been used for tepee lodge poles, and some of the larger ones for log cabins, fences and gates. We searched all over the mountain collecting dead fall, gathering them from several spots to get just the right sizes for the sweat lodge.

While gathering the wood, Joe Iron Man asked me if I understood what had happened in the ceremony the previous night. I told him "No." He repeated to me again that the grandfathers and the Creator had told him to show me the directions for the sacred pipe ceremony. I was surprised because I hadn't expected to learn the medicine ways. I was only seeking help for myself and family.

As we continued gathering wood, I was about to pull some deadfall from a gully when Joe stopped me and said, "Watch out for the wasp's nest." I hadn't noticed it. Joe, like those living on the reservation, was very aware of everything around him. His eyes missed nothing.

We loaded up the truck with logs to heat the forty sacred stones for the sweat lodge. These stones are eight to twelve inches in diameter. The logs were from four to six inches in diameter. We cut them into six-foot lengths.

After returning from the mountain about noon, we rested and ate before preparing the sweat lodge in the late afternoon. We stacked the logs in criss-cross rows—north to south, east to west. A pile was formed about five-foot square, by three-foot high, and the stones were placed on top of the platform.

The structure was very solid, but stacked so it could breathe when the flames came up through the logs to heat the stones. We brought them into the lodge later. We lit the logs on the west side where the sun sets, which is Joe Iron Man's way.

The rocks became so hot they nearly became transparent. The blazing fire eventually rose eight to twelve feet high. The gray mountain stones turned red, then yellow red. As the logs burned, the sacred stones started working their way down to grandmother earth by falling through the burning logs.

It was July and a drought year in Montana. There were forest fires everywhere. All firefighters from the reservations were out manning fire lines. As our own fire grew, we talked about how funny it would be if one of the fire-fighting planes dumped water on our fire thinking it was the start of another forest fire.

The purification ceremony began. The Holy Man brought in the first Sacred Stones from the fire outside with a pitchfork— seven in all. Each stone was sprinkled with cedar. Prayers were said for each stone, in each direction, north, south, east, and west. When the stones were needed, we brought in four or five more. It began getting warm, and I could smell the smoking cedar. It felt good. We were cast in darkness except for the flickering light of the cedar on the glowing stones when we closed the entrance flap to the sweat lodge. Small lights from the rocks danced and moved about until the Holy Man threw the first water on them. The breath of the sacred stones spewed hot steam, and I started to take in breath but couldn't. Panic engulfed my body. Eventually I calmed down and took small breaths. The Holy Man started singing and chanting, and we joined him. He threw more water. As it got hotter and hotter I became humbler and humbler. I could feel my strength and arrogance disappearing.

I prayed and sang simultaneously. I felt like I was in the womb of mother earth, protected and suffering. The sweat was streaming off my body. Joe threw more water on the rocks. More singing. Four songs were sung in the first round. Then the darkness came all around me as the first set of rocks cooled and their light went out. The light and fresh air came in after we opened the flap of the lodge. Coolness. We had just gone through the first door of purification. Three more to go. We didn't have a rock carrier, so I crawled out, clockwise, according to the instructions. I headed to the left of the sacred mound.

I took the pitchfork and brought ten more rocks from the outside fire to the Holy Man. He took them with deer antlers and placed them in the hole in the center of the sweat lodge, which represented the center of the universe.

Then I assumed my place back in the lodge and the second round began. Four songs were sung for each round. I began to feel cleansed both in body and spirit. Each time I went in and out of the sweat lodge I said "all my relations," which is customary at the beginning and end of a sweat lodge ceremony because of the deep connection to our ancestors.

We used Joe Iron Man's sacred pipe in the third round. The pipe was filled with tobacco before the sweat lodge ceremony began. Then the pipe was lit by the sweet grass which was lit by the last of the heated rocks we carried in. The smoke carried our prayers to the Creator. After the pipe ceremony, we closed the flap and entered the fourth round. Throughout the ceremony, I tried to remain sitting upright. At one point during the fourth and last door, Joe told me to lie down. He seemed to see my physical suffering through the darkness in the sweat lodge. When the ceremony was over, we went outside, took cold water, and dumped it on our bodies to close the pores and strengthen our hearts. My heart was beating so hard that I felt the pulse of the earth. The sodas we drank tasted better than at any other time I can remember.

Later Joe explained directions for the sacred pipe in a private ceremony between the two of us. He said he hoped I would use them in a good way to help others. He told me that every spring I should tie two yards of red cotton cloth in an isolated mountain location to reaffirm my directions.

After this sacred pipe ceremony, I began to see my path and my people through different eyes. I realized I had inherited a very rich heritage and spiritual path. It now all felt very natural to me, like I belonged—a feeling I had never before experienced. Being of mixed blood, I always felt like an outsider among Native Americans and non-Indians. After I became a pipe keeper, I realized that the amount of blood you had either way made no difference. It was the spirit that guided you. The directions Joe Iron Man gave me that day are a part of the ceremonies I do today.

Because of this experience, my course in life became helping others on their life's paths through prayer with the sacred pipe and with seminars that teach the Native American way.

As a young child my grandmother had sent me to a fundamentalist church, where I learned to memorize verses from the Bible. I never found my spirituality there.

Throughout my high school years, my closest friends were Catholic and I went to church with them. The services were in Latin. Although I liked the sounds, I couldn't understand the words. It seemed like a good place to pray. When I entered the U.S. Air Force and had to fill out a form naming my religious preference, I didn't know what to put down. I asked my friend what he was. He said Methodist, and that is what I wrote. Today, I would simply write, Native American Spirituality.

To me, Native American spiritualism is not a religion or an organized system of faith and worship. It is a way of life—a path. It teaches reverence for mother earth and thankfulness to all who inhabit it. Many of our ceremonies and rituals are performed to give thanks to the earth and sky for sustaining us. When we eat meat, we give thanks to the creature that provided us with nourishment. When we pick sage, we leave tobacco in thanks to the Creator for providing it. We give thanks to the Creator as we walk through our path each day in celebration of life.

It is the Native American's profound reverence for life that is so surprising to most non-Indians. I believe it was this reverence that drew me to my heritage. I believe it is this heritage, along with our environmental concerns, that has roused the curiosity of many non-Indians about the Native American way.

In this book, I share my knowledge and experience to help others learn about the Native Amerian culture and spiritual beliefs. I will show that one need not go to a reservation, take part in a medicine wheel, or have a vision quest to incorporate the Native American way into one's life.

WORLD VIEW OF EARLY NATIVE AMERICANS

Columbus and other early explorers praised the Indian way of life. The simplicity and humbleness of the Native Americans, as well as their reverence for other living things, impressed other cultures and nations.

As word of Native American life in the 1700s spread to other continents, the philosophers became intrigued with people living harmoniously with nature.

In *Discourse on Inequality*, written by the French philosopher and writer Jean Jacques Rousseau in the eighteenth century, the American Indians are praised for their love of freedom, equality and diversity. Arrell Morgan Gibson wrote in *The American Indian*: "Felix Cohen, late international authority on Native American law and polity, has stated that 'American democracy, freedom and tolerance are more American than European and have deep aboriginal roots in our land.' The

Native American example of self-determination and local sovereignty 'undoubtedly played a strong role in helping to give the colonist new sets of values that contributed to turning them from Europeans into freedom-loving Americans.' And it is out of a rich Native American democratic tradition that the distinctive political ideals of American life emerged including the practice of treating leaders 'as servants of the people instead of as their masters,' and the 'insistence that the community must respect the diversity of men and the diversity of their dreams.' "

As different ethnic and cultural groups today in America strive for equality, I'm reminded of how every person in a Plains tribe is honored and respected for his or her endowments. When a woman chose to be a warrior, although very few of them did, she had that choice. She had to prove herself, though, in the field as a hunter and warrior.

A man could be accepted when he chose to follow the woman's way. These men performed the woman's daily chores, including caring for children of the tribe. Native Americans believed these men, transvestites, possessed certain powers. Warriors came to them for special medicine for battle. Some had the gift of prophecy for the tribe or band. They were called "Winktes" by the Sioux, "Berdashe" by others. They were never discriminated against or banished from society.

Native American arts, from pottery to architecture, have permeated American culture. Most early Indian art was functional and found on everything from shields to moccasins. Later they also made objects for aesthetic value to sell to the white man. Many of these early art pieces are displayed in museums today, including Indian jewelry, quill, bead, and leather work.

Some of our most famous authors and philosophers, from N. Scott Momaday, the Kiowa-Cherokee Pulitzer Prize winning author of *House Made of Dawn*, to humorist Will Rogers, have greatly contributed to and enriched the lives of other cultures throughout the world.

These diverse talents and accomplishments have maintained for the Native American a direct link to the universe and to their spiritual roots. Their ceremonies and rituals, laced with the recognition of the individual, remind them of their heritage and spiritual nature—no matter how simple or complex their lives become. It reminds them of their unity with the animals, waters, rocks, and earth, as well as their families and ancestors. Their ceremonies pay homage to the Creator who knows them all.

A LOOK AT NATIVE AMERICANS TODAY

Native Americans today are strengthening their lives through education, and advancing themselves by learning the law of the land. They are working in science, medicine, space exploration programs, and making careers of the military. They are obtaining bachelor and master's degrees as well as Ph.D's; and they are becoming doctors and lawyers. Just a few short years ago, a bachelor's degree was uncommon because many elders considered the white man's education as arrogant. As a result, younger Native American generations were held back from achieving the materialistic goals of the white man: wealth, prestige and prominence in society.

Yet, I know how things have changed when I think of the great achievement of a Lakota elder and friend, Christine. She was well-versed in the old ways, and skilled at bead work and making ceremonial moccasins. Christine used the brass end of a shotgun shell for a thimble. In her late seventies, she earned a bachelor degree in social welfare at California State University, Long Beach. She wore an eagle feather in her cap at the graduation ceremonies.

I also have great respect for those elderly Native Americans who leave their familiar surroundings to share information in their native tongue for the betterment of their people. For example, at a class in Federal Indian law at California State University–Long Beach, a Navajo elder woman, who had never been off the reservation, came to speak to us. She spoke in her native tongue about some problems at the Hopi/Navajo reservation at Big Mountain Four Corners. She was humble, extremely neat, and dressed in traditional native clothes of velvet and leather with beautiful silver jewelry. As is the custom of many Native Americans, she kept her eyes downcast, and looked up only occasionally. A class member translated for her, since she spoke no English. She led us in prayer after her talk.

Although we have slowly assimilated into another culture and world, many of our old ways stay with us. Most Native Americans have strong ties to their families, although many have fallen off the Red Path through alcohol and drugs. We still believe in the extended family with aunts, uncles, and grandparents living under the same roof. The elders are respected, listened to, and honored. Our children are comfortable sharing a room with siblings and are taught by members of their extended family. The entire family praises the children when they are good, and ignores them when they are bad. In the traditional Native American family, children are not abused.

Many Native Americans have a difficult time dealing with the exchange of money. It's not a priority in their lives. What has significance are the objects that money can buy. I believe our fear of money is based on an old belief that it is easy to lose money and, therefore, it has no real meaning. The potlatch attitude of giving gifts is still with us. Often, when someone admires something of mine, I'll give it to them—even if I'm wearing it.

In the spring, many Native Americans who live in the city return to their reservations for spiritual renewal and family visits. Many travel hundreds of miles. It is as if we are returning to the womb of mother earth—to a safe haven, to a place where we can recapture our love and awe for the Creator's world. In regenerating our spirit and connections to our roots, we can then go back to our lives.

II

BASIC BELIEF
AND WAYS OF THE
NATIVE AMERICAN TRADITION

▲

Native Americans have a wealth of traditions. Part of this tradition is the right of the individual to incorporate his or her own ideas, and ways of interpreting Native American beliefs, into their view of their personal path.

BREATH

Without trying and sometimes without knowing, we are still part of every living thing. The universe is alive, and so is everything in it. All have the impulse of life, the flow of breath. Other traditions and religions place importance on the spirituality of breath. Breath is life and people instinctively know this.

When we sneeze, our breath leaps out momentarily. This is regarded as an omen by some cultures. Ancient and primitive people thought danger was imminent when a person sneezed—thus the terms, "Gesundheit," "God help you," or "God bless you." Breath is who and what we are, and all around us is the life breath.

The Native American links the spirit with the breath. The vocabulary of the early Indians does not contain profanity similar to "swear words" of the English language. We believe when we swear or use fowl words of hate, gossip, or lust, we dirty our spirit which rides on our breath. Our spirit goes with our last breath when we die, and this shows us the importance of the spirit that rides on our breath.

Those who wanted to show anger toward an enemy, disapproval of an action, or simply frustration when they did something like stub a toe, made loud animal sounds like a bear or other creatures.

SPIRITS

Just as we have beliefs about breath, we also have them for the spirit which we honor in ceremony and ritual.

We have great respect for our ancestors because they are the seed of our flesh. The spirits of our grandfathers, grandmothers, aunts, and uncles may be felt around us, sometimes more potently in sorrow or loss. We can also feel them more strongly, too, in joy and strength. We never know exactly who and where they are, or when and where we'll meet them, but we would not be here without our ancestors. We believe what we are today, and what we will be tomorrow, is associated with our ancestors.

We also believe there is only room for one spirit in your body. You can have other spirits around your spirit, but only one belonging to you. Perhaps those who have split, or multiple personalities have more than one spirit competing for the body host. When people are confused about their sexuality they may also have more than one spirit to contend with.

Alcohol or drugs confuse the spirit that rides on one's breath. That's why most medicine people don't use alcohol or drugs any time. When a pregnant woman uses drugs, alcohol or tobacco, we believe she is interfering with the path of the child she is carrying. We also believe that a father's drinking habits affect the unborn child's spirit.

Spirits may be felt when gentle breezes pass around us as our body moves, and when we dance, hunt, run, or make love.

Good medicine brings forth the sweet spirits and helps get rid of the sour ones in the circle. When we pray, we ask the Creator to keep us on a good path and in sweet spirit.

Many Native Americans lost contact with their animal spirits since leaving their natural outdoor environment. We once believed, and some still do, that the spirits of animals such as the buffalo, elk, bear, and winged creatures possess supernatural powers.

Many people have certain animals they call on for medicine and strength. They select one according to the qualities that the animal embodies and exemplifies. For example, one may choose the mountain lion when they need cunning and strength. One may prefer the rabbit when they need to burrow underground and retreat from the world. And after retreating for a time, they may then need the spirit of the wolverine who is known to face any problem fearlessly.

Each animal has its own special medicine that might be needed in encountering obstacles in life that force us to shift and change. In this respect, Native Americans take on the spirit of different animals for different situations. As human beings, we have the gift of change and can adapt and blend with surroundings.

Many Native Americans also feel they have spirit helpers that protect and guide them on their paths. These spirits can be animals, ancestors, or mystical entities such as the thunderbird. For example, a person might be walking down the street in a specific direction, and then get an intuitive feeling and change directions. They might attribute this feeling to a personal spirit guide. We don't always know who or what the spirit helper is. I believe we not only have good spirit helpers, but we also have negative spirits who are there to test and challenge us with the lure of the negative path. Since the universe has both positive and negative energies, so do we.

PRAYING

Most Native Americans ask the Creator for a good life, and good health for themselves. We don't ask for a new man or woman in our life, or for material things like a new car, a house, or more money, because the Creator is all knowing and already knows what we require. If we ask for specific things, besides good life and good health, there is always the danger that we'll get them, and lose something else.

Our prayers are short and simple. We pray for others first, and ourselves last. If we are praying about a world problem, the prayer might be longer. We also might pray for the Creator to help a particular person.

Many Native Americans believe that when a person who has used the spiritual path in a wrong and harmful way dies, they will wander in a negative and barren afterworld until someone takes pity on them and prays on their behalf.

This reminds me of a story told to me by a pipe keeper of the Lakota tradition. A Lakota Holy Man wondered what happened to people who were always taking medicine and artifacts that didn't belong to them. Through a vision quest, he traveled into the afterworld. He found himself in the land of nothingness and emptiness, with no feeling of hot or cold. It was like a barren desert. In the distance he saw a person coming toward him carrying a large bag over his shoulder. When they met, he asked the person what had happened. The person said that in a previous life on earth he grabbed other people's medicine and hoarded artifacts such as pipes, shields, or feathers, and used them in a wrong way.

When the Holy Man asked what the person felt, he said that he felt nothing. He lacked desire and hunger, and wandered aimlessly carrying his burden. He asked the Holy Man if people would pray for him, because then the Creator might release his spirit from his burden.

We give thanks when we pray, such as, "Thank you Creator for getting me through the darkness of night." Or during the day if something happens to us that isn't good, we thank the Creator for it not being worse. We thank grandmother earth for birth and the harvest, especially after a harsh winter or a drought.

I don't believe that spirituality is put into you. I believe it is something that already exists inside you and is brought out. Prayer helps in this process.

DIRECTIONS

"Directions" are north, east, south, west, up and down. To Native Americans, however, they are also instructions for our path and involve a certain way of doing ceremony and ritual. We all have our own directions, road or path, to follow.

The grandfathers sit in the four directions. We call on the grandfathers in the east, where the sun comes up; in the south, where the moon is; in the west, where the sun goes down; and in the north, where the grandfathers sit in darkness.

The four winds and the four seasons are directions. The four races of people are in the four directions. I believe the red man is from the west, the yellow man is from the east, the white man comes from the north, and the black man is from the south.

When early Native Americans set up their lodges in which to live, depending on the direction of the winds, they ideally placed the opening to greet the morning sun in the east.

SACRED CIRCLE

The Native American believes everything is connected in circular fashion. Circles can be from infinite to minute. Your thought or circumstance is the only thing limiting the size of the circle. All creation has its own circle without beginning or end.

As individuals, we are the center of our own circle. When the circles of other creatures are broken or destroyed, our circle is also damaged because they all overlap and affect one another. For example, take an area in Northern Canada where the caribou, the wolf, the raven, and the mouse coexist. They are in a circle. While the wolf and the raven are waiting for the migration of the caribou, which takes place twice a year, the mouse takes up the gap in the food chain. As the caribou come down from the north, the wolves deliberately run them to cull out the weak and sick. This keeps the caribou herd strong. After the wolves stuff themselves, the ravens clean up the scraps. To further illustrate the overlapping of circles, we explore how the caribou feeds on lichen moss on the way down from the north, and what it takes for the lichen to survive.

When an unknown force interrupts the delicate balance of this circle—such as man killing wolves for pelts or sport—he creates a break in the circle. When the wolf population depletes, the mice get out of control. Caribou lose their strength by breeding with the weaker ones that survived being killed by the wolves. The raven has nothing to clean up, goes hungry, and moves on to another area leaving the first area barren.

Those four creatures aren't the only animals affected. Creatures throughout all the migratory area suffer. For example, when the caribou herd migrates south or returns north, they take their sick and weak in tow. They mate and weaken the herd for future migrations. Ultimately, many or all die. The natives who rely on that particular food source find it diminished or gone. The depleted herd doesn't deposit its usual amount of waste along the migratory trail, which affects plant growth (another overlapping circle) in those areas.

By interfering with the circles and destroying this delicate balance, man ultimately loses because we no longer live in an unbroken circle.

Each time living things fall and disappear before us, all circles of life are affected. I become filled with fear and sadness when I see the broken and sometimes empty circles we have created for ourselves and future creation.

Fortunately, like the Phoenix struggling to be reborn from the ashes, millions of people throughout the world are working together to mend these broken circles, and to heal mother earth. As we gain knowledge about our environment and endeavor to restore it, we not only begin to heal our own circle but other circles as well.

While up at the Fort Belknap reservation in Montana, I was gathering sage with some children. Afterwards, I took them to a swimming hole called "big warm," which is fed by a natural hot spring. I noticed in the distant sky, an eagle circling, working its way toward the mountains behind me. In the distance, what I thought was another eagle circling in the same path, turned out to be one of the largest hawks I'd ever seen. Both the eagle and hawk were in the same hunting path, circling in unison about a mile apart from one another. I was reminded of the circle of life.

The Native American also understood time as cyclical and circular rather than linear because their entire concept of life is circular. Everything has a natural order. Patience brings that order into the circle. Because of this, Native Americans have had a difficult time adjusting to the linear deadlines of non-Indian society.

Native Americans have many ways to visualize the sacred circle. Some do it with a medicine wheel of personal colors, animals and plants, or rocks represented in specific areas of a wheel. I don't use a medicine wheel because I believe we are the center of our own circle that is limitless and never ending.

We don't make the circle. The circle is made for us by the Creator.

HOUSING

Housing for most Native Americans means circular structures. We believe that the spiritual flow of life can be interrupted by corners and that the negative parts of life live in corners. Our circular tepee represents the universe.

As a young boy, I heard old white men laughing as they talked about how the government had built prefab houses for the Indians, only to find them living in a tepee or hogan behind the house. They had turned the house over to their cattle, chickens, and hogs because they were more comfortable living in the more circular tepee or hogan.

To make the traditional square homes we live in today circular, we burn sage, sweet grass, or cedar in a clockwise motion in each room. This purifies the corners and symbolically places the home in a sacred circle.

SHIELDS

Shields were circular and a symbol of the sacred circle. There are four types including a lightweight dance shield, a medicine or Holy Man's shield, a warrior's shield, and sometimes a miniature replica of the warrior's shield.

The warrior's shield was the main part of his war regalia and medicine. It was used in battle to deflect arrows, lances, and even bullets. Usually it was made from the hump of the sacred buffalo, which is the thickest part of the hide. Other shields, used in dance and by Holy Men, were thinner and often made of elk and deer hide. Images of sacred visions were painted on the shields. Sometimes feathers, medicine bags, and ermine tails were added to them. These warriors earned their shields from early boyhood training in the ways of war and hunting.

Shields were also used in the ghost dances that originated as a form of medicine in the late 1800s. The vision of the ghost dance was first received by a Piute Indian named Wovoka from Nevada. The Indians believed the dance would return the sacred buffalo and lands to them.

Those who danced made themselves "ghost shirts" painted with prayer symbols such as birds, stars, moons, and animals, to protect them from harm by non-Indians. The dance spread like wildfire. The whites overreacted because of recent Indian wars and this led to the Wounded Knee Massacre. The massacre stopped the dance, and killed the spirit of the Native American, leaving them to the reservation and abject misery and despair.

I don't know of any Native Americans on the reservation today who still make shields.

LAND

To Native Americans, the Creator owns the land and we are only borrowing it. When the white man first negotiated for land, the Native American thought he was giving them gifts for permission to hunt or cross into their areas. The Native American did not have a concept of land ownership. For them the land was put there by the Creator for use while the person, band or tribe lived there. When the Native American learned the meaning of the word, "land ownership," the wars began.

The Native American always had an area of land that they didn't call their own, but which was used for hunting, farming, fishing, and gathering. If possible they stayed in one place and lived off that area in a balanced manner, using no more than was needed to sustain the group. When other tribes crossed into that area, it caused disputes. The other tribes would be chased out because the existing tribe felt the land would support only a specific number of people. Any more would upset the balance. If the encroaching tribe persisted because they could no longer survive on the lands where they had been living, both tribes would meet to work out agreements that would benefit all.

When the white man began infringing on the land, they moved the tribes to barren lands where they could not sustain themselves. Thus many tribes had to move to new locations that were often already occupied by bands who resented the added encroachment. Thus the conflicts between tribes increased.

Due to this history with the white man, many Native Americans today whose lives have been spent on reservations still hold bad memories. However, a growing number of Native Americans are working within the system to right some of the wrongs that took place at an earlier time. They are doing this while still maintaining the rich heritage of the Native American.

COLORS

Native Americans are very colorful. Their clothing, utensils, housing, ceremony, and body decorations reflect the natural beauty that surrounded them.

Specific colors carry certain meanings which vary among tribes and medicine people. The same color takes on different meanings for the individual. We use the color or colors that are right for our own medicine or decoration.

Some medicine people incorporate colors into their healing ceremonies. Some have only one color, like myself. Others have four or more colors. They can receive their colors through visions, during ceremony, and from instructions given by a Holy Man.

I was given the color red by the Holy Man, Joe Iron Man, and I respected that choice. He also instructed me not to use black in ceremony. Some tribes, though, use black because they believe they should recognize the negative in ceremony.

NAMES

Native Americans refer to God as Creator, Father, Holy One, Great Spirit, and All Sacred, among others. The Cree and Algonquian refer to the Creator as Manitou. The Iroquois use Orenda, and the Lakota Sioux, Wakan Tanka. All holy names are revered. I prefer the term "the Creator" because it stands for creation and is both male and female.

The Native American originally got the label "Indian" from Columbus who thought he had landed on the coast of East India. The natives his men encountered were, therefore, called "Indians."

Native American is a more common term used today. Many Native Americans take offense at being called "Indian," or other names such as "Chief."

On a personal level, Native Americans adopt many names for themselves. Some get their names in jest as children. Others get them lovingly from family and friends in a way that is similar to how non-Indians bestow a pet name on friends and lovers. Names were also given for deeds in hunting or war. Although names were never given to hurt feelings, an exception to this were the names given an enemy of another tribe.

A man carrying a name like "Bear's Arm" might refer to the man's medicine. Or "Eyes in the Back of His Head" could mean that his senses were so in tune that he could "feel" someone in back of him.

Sometimes young children received funny names like Hopping Rabbit because an adult or playmate saw the child hopping like a rabbit. Nicknames are kept only until the child reaches puberty.

The child's original or received name is usually given by a person of the same sex who has prayed to a spirit and received a vision on behalf of the godchild, according to Robert H. Lowie, author of *Indians of the Plains*.

Other means of acquiring names include:

▲ From a warrior experience.
▲ A new name given by a medicine man after an illness.
▲ In honor of a relative or friend.
▲ By a vision or dream.

Native Americans don't take their names lightly, regardless of how it sounds since it has come to them through a natural or spiritual way.

Many people believe it is necessary to get a Native American name to be on a path. I don't think it's necessary to search deliberately for such a name or to have one. If one comes to you, it will happen in its own way and time.

Another medicine person once jokingly called me "Half Human," because of my mixed heritage. I tried to think which part was human and which part was not. Those with a Native American heritage prefer to be called "half-bloods," rather than "half-breed." Only animals breed.

MUSIC

Songs are a part of our spiritual, supernatural, and day-to-day world. They reflect our many moods and increase the power of our medicine. Every ceremony has songs; the sacred pipe, sweat lodge, sun dance, powwow, death, war and harvesting. We have songs for tobacco, healing, humor and for nearly everything we do.

Songs undergo changes constantly and are exchanged between tribes. Sometimes tribal songs are bartered to others who need that medicine.

Any occasion can bring forth a song. Mothers sing lullabies to their babies in traditional native tongue. We have the old traditional songs and the personal ones made up on the spot that follow the traditional ways. A song may contain one line to convey a message to the grandfathers, grandmother earth, or the Creator. We chant in song in our native tongue and sometimes accompany it with drum, like a singing prayer.

Drums keep the rhythm of the heart beat. Beating a drum may be a natural instinct, just as we tap a pencil on a desk, or run a stick down a picket fence. Yet it takes on greater meaning to the Native American. The drum is considered a gift from the Creator. Many believe it projects the sound of thunder.

The drum is an instrument that comes in many sizes and shapes. Drums used in powwows are made in a ceremonial way with care, prayers and smudging. Most are made of a rawhide surface on top and bottom, with wood on the sides. The stick used to beat the drum is usually covered with a leather head. Drums can be placed on or suspended off the ground, or hand-held. Some drums are filled with water and used by the singer to make a variety of sounds.

The drum beat stays in tune with the body's rhythm and heartbeat, no matter how fast or slow it is going. Many songs that are out of rhythm with our bodies can create disorder in the spirit, body, and mind. Just as excessively loud music can damage the ears, music not in tune with the body's natural flow can damage the spirit.

Men who beat the drum at powwows are called "singers." I have been at powwows where the Northern Plains singers, who are usually higher pitched and louder than most, were really going loud and strong. I noticed a small baby sleeping contentedly through the drumming while the singers and dancers were performing.

Occasionally I pick up my hand-held drum and beat the drum and sing. It helps let loose some of my frustrations, and balances me. Sometimes I just beat it to hear the beautiful sound, other times to make noise. It often brings out the child in me. Playing the drum feels healthy and very healing.

Indian Drum

Procreation . . . Tandem power
Mistletoe living from the blood of the pine
Four legged hear the beat of the Indian drum.
The heartbeat of the great Earth Mother
Eco-balanced in the fragile web of time

Tender power achieved by surrender
To the Great Mystery of all things
Animals hear the drum of the woman totem
Tiny singers of the forest salute the sacred sunrise
Dancing in the light of this moment forever

Ghosts of last night's rain steam from the forest floor
As they carry scents of sage and pine and dreams
To the grateful daughter souls of early autumn.
The seekers of the vision of the future of our people
Are gathered here upon the sacred ground

A revival nation seeking ancient wisdom
From Nature's mighty forces of the mountain
They counseled with old ones from the faraway
Who walked among these boulders, pines and redwoods
And saw the green against the same blue sky

Whispers sweet as wood smoke to the senses
Curled through the shadows of the dreamers visions
In answer to the drum beat of the seekers
Walk barefoot with respect upon the earth
All things in abundance shall come from the great sky

Fran Dancing Feather
Big Bear City, California

Flutes (or flageolet) are widely used for expressing romantic love by different tribes. They are usually made from wood, approximately 16–24 inches long and 1–2 inches in diameter with about eight finger holes. Sometimes a carved bird or other effigy is tied on with leather to be used as a sliding reed.

The Indian flute, often played during courting, provides a low, soothing and loving sound. It can be almost hypnotic. When a young man played the flute to call his intended loved one, she would recognize its sound letting her know of his interest, and that his heart was hers.

The flute is also used for entertainment and relaxation. Other wind instruments, such as hollow eagle bone whistles, are used in ceremonies like the Sun or Thunder Dances. Sometimes at powwows other bird wing bones are used such as the loon, or turkey. Also, some whistles are designed in the shapes of water birds.

Rattles are used in healing ceremonies for needed prayers to call in the spirits. They are made from a variety of hollowed out gourds or taut rawhide, and filled with pebbles, sand, beads, small bones, or dried corn.

Some medicine people look for a large ant hill to find small stones and tiny fossil bones that the ants brought up from the earth when building their mounds. They put these artifacts in the rattles.

Sometimes rattles will contain up to 405 pieces of the stones and fossils to represent the numbers of herb combinations used in healing by some medicine people.

NUMBERS

Numbers have always played a significant part in Native American life. They were very exacting in the numbers of "things" used in ceremony—such as the specific number of rocks used in the different sweat lodge ceremonies, or the numbers of herbs used in healing and other ceremonies. They also watched for the number of animals leaving an area to herald the coming of winter.

In addition to their general use, some specific numbers have additional meaning. Four is one of the most sacred numbers used by Native Americans. During the pipe ceremony, we honor the grandfathers who sit in the four directions. Up to forty stones are used in the sweat lodge, and 104 rocks are used in the healing sweat. A medicine bundle may contain four times four things. Four tufts of buffalo hair symbolized the four-legged animals. The bundle can contain four kinds of skins from animals, four types of bird feathers, four kinds of plants, and four kinds or colors of rocks and stones.

Many aspects of life are seen in terms of four: the four elements of the universe: the four directions, seasons, and races. We also see things in pairs, which we consider a part of the natural order.

According to Native American thought, man strives to possess the four virtues of bravery, generosity, endurance, and wisdom. Women strive to possess bravery, generosity, truthfulness and the ability to bear children. Women avoid the men's camp for four days when they are menstruating (of the moon), or after giving birth.

Peter T. Furst notes in *Hallucinogens and Culture* that part of the Navaho ritual for pipe making involves the singing of four songs by pipe makers after making each pipe. The pipes are then dried for four days. Each pipe is painted one of the four colors in respect to the four sacred directions.

Following a death in a tribe some Plains Indians wait until the fourth night to feast, use a ceremonial pipe, or to offer food to the spirits.

BODY DECORATIONS

Many tribes were noted for their practice of tattooing, including the Plains Cree. It was used to decorate the body, enhance beauty, and for good medicine.

One method rarely used by the Cree was to pass an awl under the skin and then to draw a piece of sinew thread covered with charcoal or soot through it. This method is considered one of the most painful ways to tattoo. Another method of tattooing used by Crees was to make small incisions with a piece of flint or other cutting material. Some tribes used natural coloring.

The Cree men were tattooed with a series of dots running in two lines under the chin and down the neck, and with four lines of dots on the chest, down the sides of the stomach, and across the arms. Cree women were tattooed only from the lower lip to the chin. This was a decorative, ceremonial, and social custom. Tattooing also showed courage, since they endured great pain and suffering doing it.

Another method of decorating the body, not permanent like tattooing, was face and body painting. Different designs and colors were painted to depict what the individual was going to do—such as preparing for a war party, getting revenge, gaining protection, or preparing for ceremony. The dead were sometimes dressed up in their full regalia with the body painted for the journey.

Horses also were decorated and painted for merit in battle from counting coup (important successful actions), killing enemy, or stealing horses or slaves.

The book, *Lame Deer Seeker of Visions*, by John (Fire) Lame Deer and Richard Erdoes, speaks of symbols and how many Native Americans believe that tattoos serve as a passport to the hereafter. Some Crees, including me, accept this belief. Lame Deer says, "The moccasins of the dead have their soles beaded in a certain way to ease the journey to the hereafter. For the same reason, most of us have tattoos on our wrists. These are not like the tattoos of your sailors: daggers, hearts and nude girls; but just a name, a few letters, or designs. The Owl Woman who guards the road to the spirit lodges looks at these tattoos and lets us pass. They are like a passport. Many Indians believe that if you don't have these signs on your body, the Ghost Woman won't let you through but will throw you over a cliff. Then you will have to roam the earth endlessly as a wanagi—a ghost. All you will be able to do is frighten people and whistle. Maybe it's not so bad being a wanagi. It could even be fun. I don't know. But, as you see, I have my arms tattooed."

ROBES AND BLANKETS

Before contact with Europeans, the Native American blankets were made from the hides of buffalo, elk, deer, wolf, rabbit and coyote. Most of the blankets (called buffalo robes by Native Americans) of the Plains people were of buffalo hide because it was the most available. Most blankets today are made of wool or cotton, the latter being the star and patch quilts.

Blankets were worn and given for many reasons by the Plains Indian. They used them not only for warmth, but to make statements about their feelings when in council and for solitude, death, love, and play. They were also used as give-aways at potlatches which were a sharing of food and ceremony with other families or tribes.

They were draped over the body like a Roman senator for council meetings. In solitude, they covered the head. In death, a body may be wrapped in a blanket. Couples sometimes wrap together in blankets, jokingly referred to as "snagging blankets." A single woman takes a blanket to a powwow, sees a bachelor who seems a little cold, and might ask, "Would you like to share my blanket?" That is Native American humor. Blankets were also used to make capotes or blanket coats, leggings, and breech cloths that barely covered the front and rear.

The Native Americans borrowed the early American pioneer's tradition of quilting and refined it for their own purposes. Most Plains tribes make star quilts. Although men traditionally make other art objects, they rarely made quilts. The women made quilts with different star shaped patterns representing the morning star. Each woman had her own pattern and it became their personal medicine. The quilting pieces are cut from old clothing and leftover scraps of material. An old blanket is often used for the lining.

In the early days, all quilts were sewn by hand. Nowadays many Native Americans make them on the sewing machine but they are just as warm. Many Native American men and women today are wrapped in these morning star quilts for burial.

My star quilt was made by a medicine woman. It has given me many days and nights of warmth and comfort. It makes me feel like Linus, the character in the Charlie Brown comic strip, who drags his blanket with him wherever he goes.

III

CEREMONIES AND RITUALS

▲

All Native American ceremonies take place in a sacred circle whether it is considered a circle of the universe, the world, the area in which we live, or a small circle of people.

Native Americans are in personal ceremony from the time they get up in the morning, until they are asleep at night. They commemorate every part of life, from birth to death, the good as well as the bad times. Celebrations are a part of life that keep us in touch with ourselves, family and friends, the earth, our Creator and the universe. It takes us away from the tasks and struggle of daily living. Without celebrations we become colorless people of burden. Even sleep can be celebrated by remembering our dreams.

Dreams are very important in the lives of most Native Americans because they are used for guidance. Dreams and visions permeate everyday life. We may purposefully put ourselves in meditation to gain a vision, or understanding of some issue or question in our life. Many writers and artists of the Native American and American tradition have attributed their works of art to personal dreams or visions. One of my dreams of the thunderbird later became reality in ceremony and perhaps had prepared me for my spiritual path.

Some of our ceremonies are a preparation to ready oneself to be heard by the Creator. We try to achieve the humbleness necessary for such times. We are no more special in the universe than any other creature, because without other creations we do not exist. We believe being humble helps us to be noticed by the Creator.

We have separate ceremonies for men and women, and many for both. They are among different tribes and go by a variety of names. They also serve a multitude of purposes: purification of the dead, rebirth, obtaining a vision, giving thanks to the Creator, creating bonds between friends, preparing boys for manhood and girls for womanhood, and feeling our connection to the universe.

Native American children are welcomed into many ceremonies. The elders are honored and encouraged to lead the ceremony in prayer. So many of us have lost our native tongue that it is a treat to hear the elders speak our sacred language.

Prayers are always said in every ceremony. In turn, the ceremony is a prayer to the Creator. When Native Americans pray, we become part of the sacred circle, and are sometimes oblivious to all that is around us. I've noticed that when our people are down on their knees on mother earth in prayer, they don't brush off the dirt when they rise. Being in ceremony is all encompassing and other thoughts don't enter. Also, the dirt is as much a part of us as the air we breathe.

We do not interrupt someone in ceremony or prayer. The person may be receiving something very special to their lives, or that of another person for whom they are praying.

Our ceremonies and rituals include the offerings of: smudging, smoking, singing and drumming, praying, ceremonial dance, thanksgiving, suffering, humbleness, and fasting.

We participate in these ceremonies and rituals to acknowledge:

Art work (including body painting and tattooing)
Potlatch
Gift-giving
Opening medicine bundles
Rebirth
Cleansing and purification

Bonding with others
Vision quest
Sun and thunder dances
Sweat lodge
Gathering sage
Honoring relations
Making tobacco prayer ties
Sacred pipe ceremonies
Purification and releasing
Cloth ceremony
Preparation for death
Becoming a warrior
Returning warriors
Drum
Healing
Puberty rituals
Dreaming
Medicine signs

SMUDGING

Native Americans use smudge (burn sage) at the beginning of most ceremonies for purification and readiness for prayer.

To smudge, first find a sea shell or other container that can hold fire and be used only for smudge burning. My personal smudge container, which travels with my sacred pipe, is an old tin sugar scoop.

Take a small amount of sage, place it in your container and light it. Once ignited blow or fan out the flame to make it smoke. With both hands opened, reach into the smoke and draw it in toward your heart and over your head. Next reach with your right hand, pull the smoke toward your left shoulder and down your arm. Then take your left hand in the same manner and pull the smoke down your right arm. Do the same for your right and left legs with the same hand movements. If you're sitting cross-legged in front of the smudge, grab some smudge for the bottom of your feet to purify the path that you have walked. This smudging completes your purification and preparation for ceremony and prayer.

Preparing a ceremonial smudge kit is a simple matter and doesn't require elaborate artifacts. Most personal prayer ceremonies can be done with just sage. Later you can add sweet grass, cedar, tobacco, and a feather for fanning the sage smoke. Although a feather is not necessary, any type will do except those that might be obtained illegally from an eagle, hawk, owl and other predatory or migratory birds. Native Americans, however, are free to use feathers from these birds for their rituals.

Some people acquire a personal prayer pipe to add to their smudge kit. A small rug can be used for an altar and a place for your pipe, smudging accoutrements, and tobacco.

VISION QUEST

The purpose of a vision quest is to give the seeker more insight and understanding about his path in life. There are many types of vision quests. One is when a Holy Man goes on a lone vision quest without the aid of others to receive answers to some of his questions, and to enrich his medicine ways. Another kind is done with the help of a Holy Man and with the support of others who keep a fire going for the vision seeker. When the vision quest is done with a Holy Man, he decides what your needs are and whether or not you require an "eternal fire." An eternal fire must be kept burning for the entire time of the quest.

The vision quest usually requires four days of fasting. The Holy Man will tell you exactly how to do your quest and you have to trust him with your life. Each seeker will be directed to his sacred circle away from other vision seekers. Most Plains Indians conduct their vision quests on a mountain or hill.

During the four days of fasting, one may stay up all night praying and holding onto their sacred pipe. When the sun comes up, perhaps one will sleep. The suffering you endure helps with the visions and makes the quest a humbling experience.

After spending four days in the mountains, the person making the quest comes down and explains everything that he has seen, heard and experienced to the Holy Man—even if it doesn't make sense. The Holy Man interprets the vision. It is important, therefore, to try to remember everything that happens, no matter how insignificant it may seem. The Holy Man may also take you into the sweat lodge to talk. Sometimes he may do half the sweat ceremony before you go up to the mountain, and the other half when you come down. Often there will be food prepared for you at the end of your quest. Sometimes your friends and family may make tobacco ties to encircle and protect you during your vision quest.

Sometimes a person seeking the vision quest will be chased off the mountain during the four day span because of fear, hunger, need for warmth, or by some of the Creator's creatures, such as a bear or coyote.

One quester said he went up to the mountain and the ants came to him. He picked up his blanket and moved to another part of his circle, but still they followed him. He tried moving to several other places in the circle, but the ants wouldn't leave him alone. He didn't complete his vision quest. There is no shame in not finishing the vision quest. It simply means the person isn't yet ready. No one ridicules the person because they know the decision is between the vision quester, the Creator, and the grandfathers.

The man's vision quest is a sacred ceremony, not to be undertaken without the help of a Holy Man. It is a serious and dangerous undertaking. People have been known to die on these quests.

Women traditionally have their own vision quest at puberty. A mentor, usually an elderly woman, instructs her in the chores she is to do for the four nights she spends alone in a small tepee. She gets little to eat. Other women of the tribe help her through this transitional period. A family celebration usually follows, with prayers and gifts. Unlike the men, these young women are not put through the same rigors of fasting and staying in an unfamiliar environment.

Many outsiders believe that Native American ceremonies are barbaric involving pain, suffering and deprivation. I consider it, in fact, inhumane and unnatural to have a ceremony that does not require suffering during periods of transition and personal growth.

Perhaps if American youth gangs had specific, healthy and productive rituals to participate in as they approached manhood, they might not have to resort to gang activities, or other machismo acts, to prove themselves and endanger others.

PRAYER TIES

Prayer ties are small cloth bags filled with tobacco. They are placed around the sacred circle that surrounds the vision quester. In certain ceremonies, such as a Lakota vision quest, up to 405 prayer ties are used to represent the 405 herb combinations used by some medicine people.

Prayer ties are also made before going into the sweat lodge, and can be made for yourself, family, or friends who need your help and prayers. One needs only about eight ties for offering in the sweat lodge and other ceremonies. Prayers are said for each individual tie, and then they are taken into the sweat ceremony. They are stuck in the willow branches on the inside roof of the lodge for acceptance and blessing by the Creator, grandfathers and grandmother earth.

To make prayer ties, first smudge yourself and then take different colors of cotton cloth and cut them into small squares of about an inch and a half. Then take a pinch of tobacco and place it in the center, and twist the neck of the bag. Next, take a continuous piece of thread, long enough to tie all the prayer bags in a line together, one at a time. As each is tied, a prayer should be said. Tie the neck of the bag by wrapping a continuous piece of thread around the bag and make a knot. I like to make four turns of the thread because of the significance of the number four. Continue making one prayer tie after another using the same string of thread until there are as many as you need. This manner of making prayer ties is a Lakota Sioux way.

SACRED PIPE AND CLOTH CEREMONY

Every spring I take two yards of red cotton cloth and tie it around a tree in the mountains to confirm myself as a pipe keeper, and to cleanse my pipe. Someone once asked me why two yards of pure cotton, and I jokingly told him it's because it takes that much to tie it around a tree.

I try to find a place in the mountains or hills not frequented by others, and look for an oak or any tree that has strong roots. I sit and face north with my sacred pipe and cloth under the tree because each direction is at my grasp in a natural, circular way. During all ceremonies I try to sit facing this way because north is where the grandfathers sit in darkness, and because north and south is the path of the thunderbird.

I lay out my altar which has the sacred pipe, tobacco, smudge and cloth, and I begin the pipe ceremony. I smudge to the same directions normally used with the pipe. Then I tie the cloth and leave it on the tree. Sometimes I rip the cloth into four equal strips and tie them on branches pointing in the four directions. Pure cotton is best because it is a natural fiber, grown from the earth.

One year I came back to the same tree I had tied three previous times and found it stripped of the cloth. Then I found small pieces of cloth scattered about the ground and realized that critters of the forest had used my offering for nesting and warmth. It warmed my heart to know that my offering was accepted by the Creator in this way.

PURIFICATION AND RELEASING CEREMONY

The cloth purification ceremony is another way of releasing the problems and burdens of life. You can do the first part of this ceremony in the privacy of your home without the burden of clothing. The second part takes place later in the mountains. Use two yards of cloth of a color that is comfortable for your feelings. I would suggest not using black. The idea is to get rid of the negative, not draw it to you.

At home, smudge yourself with sage and then fold the cloth. Using both hands, rotate the cloth clockwise over the smudge. Point it first to the east, then to the south, west and north, saying a prayer in each direction.

Next point the cloth to grandmother earth, raise it slightly to the fire, raise it a little farther to the smudge, and then point it straight up to the Creator. You can ask for release from any problems you have, and can pray for good health and a good life. While you are doing this first part of the ceremony, concentrate on placing your troubles and woes on the cloth. This is a personal ceremony.

Next, unfold the cloth and drape it over the top of your head and pull it around your shoulders. Add more sage to your smudging. Take one hand and pull the smudge toward your heart, and up over your head. Continue smudging yourself with sage while talking to the Creator about your problems. Eventually you may feel sticky and sweaty as the cloth absorbs your negativities. After you feel you have released your problems and negative feelings, the ceremony is complete. Remove the cloth and fold it. Save the ashes from the burned sage. Put the cloth and ashes away until you find time to go to a comfortable, quiet place in the mountains or hills to tie your cloth on a tree. This is the second part of the ceremony. Sprinkle the ashes at the base of the tree, say a small prayer, and tie the cloth in a clockwise direction. If you find a tree with limbs going in the four directions, tear the cloth in four equal parts and tie one strip on each limb. Thank the Creator, leave it and walk away.

PIPE CEREMONY

Most Plain's Indian ceremonies and rituals call for the sacred pipe ceremony. Different Native American tribes use other types of ceremonial pipes.

A pipe keeper is considered a medicine person. Like Holy Men or healers (who have their own functions), pipe keepers don't usually drink alcohol or take drugs. Since it takes four days or longer to work alcohol or drugs out of our system, during that four days of cleansing, the sacred pipe cannot be used in any ceremonies. When I do a pipe ceremony, I ask those who have had a drink that day not to participate.

Women in their moon (menstrual period) don't participate either, since it is believed they possess a different power at this time. Since husbands and wives are considered to be bonded in all phases of their lives, spouses also do not take part in ceremony during their wives' moon. I consider, too, that when women are in their moon, they are already in a sacred ceremony associated with creation.

The words, "all my relations," are sometimes used in ceremony since whatever we do affects our living family and those who have gone before us.

I conduct all my ceremonies clockwise because of the "felt" sense that the earth is rotating on its axis in that direction. In the Northern Hemisphere, the sense that the earth is turning clockwise occurs because as the sun moves east to west it dips to the south and creates that impression. The opposite "felt" sense occurs in the Southern Hemisphere. In reality, the earth rotates on its axis around the sun in a counterclockwise direction. If we were to view the North Pole from outer space, the earth would appear to be spinning counterclockwise, but if viewing it from the South Pole from outer space, it would appear to be spinning clockwise. The same is true of the moon.

The orbit of the sun within the Milky Way galaxy is counterclockwise, and the motion of our galazy from earth isn't known.

If I were to do a pipe ceremony counterclockwise, it would feel negative. Clockwise to me is positive. Yet, others do ceremonies counterclockwise, and it is a positive and valid way to them.

My pipe ceremonies are never performed perfectly. There is always a mistake. I don't do it on purpose. It just happens and becomes part of the ceremony. Only the Creator is perfect.

BLESSING CENTERS AND DWELLINGS

A medicine person is often called on to bless a new Native American center or clinic. These ceremonies include simple smudging, or the sacred pipe. Afterwards, participants share food. I have heard of centers not having ceremony before opening and they never seemed to function well.

Before Native Americans move into new homes, the places are smudged. Although most Native Americans smudge frequently once in their homes, it is still good to have the blessing of a medicine person occasionally because of the problems and negativities that arise in the normal routine of life. Some occupants smudge the house and themselves after having guests who may have brought negativity there.

CEREMONY FOR HEALING

Another type of ceremony done by a pipe keeper involves prayers for healing, but is not the same as that done by a Holy Man or Woman. For example, a woman came to me about two years ago during a seminar on Native American spirituality that I was teaching in Riverside, California. She told me of a young neighbor who was in a coma following his fall from a tree. He had suffered severe head injuries. The parents, who were not Native American, had asked her to see if I would do prayers for the boy. They brought tobacco, which is the accepted offering for the Creator, to be given to the pipe keeper. The entire class took part in the boy's prayer ceremony. The next day the prayers were answered. He came out of the coma.

Often the greater the numbers of people praying in sincerity and humbleness, the stronger the medicine.

DEATH: PASSING OVER

Native Americans have a variety of beliefs about death. In the old days, many believed that if you buried a person above ground it allowed the Creator to find their spirits more easily. So, burials took place by cremation on a scaffold, or letting nature take its course on the scaffold without cremation. Some Native Americans use interment, or place the body in a tree. Sometimes an elder will simply go off to die if they feel they want to spare their tribe the burden of suffering with them.

Our choices for burial these days are limited because of laws and restrictions. Tightly sealed coffins are traditional burials for non-Indians. Their bodies cannot be devoured by other creatures, nor can they seep out onto grandmother earth from where they came. Sharing our body with grandmother earth seems like a good idea to Native Americans. We believe it is our spirits, not our bodies, that may take on new life elsewhere.

One Lakota Holy Man told me that he wanted to be cremated so that he wouldn't be dug up by the curious like many of his ancestors, and end up in some cold museum.

I talked to another elder, a Blackfoot, who lives in Southern California. He told me that every time he went to the hospital they tried to keep him there for observation and treatment. They took his clothes and made him put on the "back-view shirt." The reason he went there was just to get his medication. When they tried to keep him, he tried to leave the hospital in the back-view shirt. The nurses caught up with him and gave him back his clothes. He wasn't going to waste the rest of his life in a hospital, he said, since the doctors told him that he had only a short time to live. He said that only he and the Creator knew when he was going to die—not the doctors. When he was ready, he said he was going to take his pipe, blanket, and, "of course my pain killers," and go up in the hills, sit up against a tree, and die. He said he hoped that when they found him they would have to scrape him off the tree.

The family of the dead often give away the deceased's belongings so the items won't remind them of their grief. In the past, they sometimes killed the man's best horse and placed it near the burial site to help the deceased person travel through the afterlife.

Many Native Americans believe in an afterlive, although not one that parallels the Christian belief in heaven. Native Americans consider death a great mystery, not a place. They believe that just before death, the relatives and friends who have already passed over visit the dying person. If you're there with the dying person, you may hear them talking to his or her deceased relations. It makes the passing easier when friendly faces are there to help you through a journey. I hope this is true because there are some people "over there" I want to talk to. Our Holy Men have journeyed through this afterlife in vision quests and have seen this other world.

Many Plains Indians believe that the owl is the messenger of death. The owl comes to the house, pecks, and makes noise at the window or door to let us know that somebody in our family is very sick or dying.

This is the reason why many Plains Indians don't use owl feathers in ceremony. Other tribes, though, look at the owl in a different way and use its feathers. Personally, I don't use owl feathers, but I believe the owl is a very special creature because of its way. Death is a part of living.

PREPARATION CEREMONY FOR DEATH

Florian (Sonnie) Velasquez, an elder in his eighties from the Morongo Reservation in California, was dying of cancer of the lungs. He requested I do a pipe ceremony for his passage.

It was an honor to be asked and I went to the reservation Monday, Oct. 10, 1988. When I arrived at his house, his family was there. I went to his room and found him lying on the bed wearing jeans. A small man, he appeared to be of a strong character, and looked like he had experienced life to the fullest. You could feel his pain by looking into his face. I removed my sacred pipe from the bag, and placed it on the foot of the bed. Mae, his oldest child, was in the room with another daughter standing at the door. The remainder of the family waited in the living room. Before handing me a cigarette for a tobacco offering, he took it between his fingers in both hands, held it up to the Creator and said a prayer.

Then he handed the tobacco offering to me and asked for the pipe ceremony, and I said, "It is my honor to do this for you."

I loaded the sacred pipe and began. When I handed the pipe to Mr. Velasquez, he couldn't smoke it because of his illness, so he touched the pipe to his right shoulder and then his left, which is the same as smoking it. You could see the pain lift from his face. The ceremony was complete after the pipe passed to Mae and back to me. In a whisper, Mr. Velasquez then asked Mae how much the ceremony would cost. Mae laughed a little and said, "Just the tobacco."

He smiled and said, "That's good." What Mr. Velasquez meant was that the old ways were still being honored—no fee. His last pipe ceremony had taken place several years previously with his people, the Shoshone, at the Wind River Reservation in Wyoming.

I gave him sweet grass and a small bag with the ashes from the ceremony, and told his son to bury them with his father to help him on his journey.

He kept the ashes and sweet grass by his side until his death. The next evening Mae called and said that twenty minutes after I left her father went into the kitchen and fixed a bite to eat. Before the ceremony the family had been bringing his food to the bedroom. The following morning, he got up, went into town and took care of business matters. Three days later Mae called and said her father had died.

RETURNING WARRIORS

In the old days when a warrior returned from battle with another tribe, or later, with the white man, he went through a cleansing ritual to return him to his good spirit. Similar ceremonies still take place today when Native Americans return from battle.

After World War II, many of our Native American soldiers came back to their reservations such as Fort Peck, Montana to be greeted by their entire tribe. The soldiers walked between two lines of family and friends to be symbolically pulled back into the folds of the tribe. The burden of war was taken off their shoulders and the blood of the enemy cleansed from their hands. This purification ceremony which included a sweat lodge, feasting, and celebration lasted for several days. The men cleansed the death, killing, and fear of war from their spirits. The Native American knows that killing another human being is not natural but, sometimes a necessity. Similar ceremonies took place in the aftermath of the Korean, Vietnam, and Persian Gulf wars.

THE THUNDER DANCE CEREMONY

The Plains Cree Thunder Dance is a prayer of thanksgiving and honors the thunder. It is the most sacred Cree ceremony.

The Holy Man usually sets up the dance ceremony and instructs the dancers. He also supervises construction of a sweat lodge, and a ceremonial arbor where the dance takes place.

A knowledegable elder directs the ceremony. No cameras, firearms, alcohol or drugs are allowed. All those who have gathered for the ceremonies stay in tents, tepees, campers, and around the outside parameters of the dance grounds, unless they live on, or close to the reservation.

The Thunder Dance usually takes place in the late spring in honor of the thunderbird who goes south in the late fall and returns in the spring for feeding when the berries are ripe. The ceremony lasts four days and usually begins on a Thursday, although I don't know of any special sabbath for Native Americans.

The Plains Cree use cloth in the Thunder Dance. They take two yards of cotton cloth and tie it on the center pole in the ceremonial arbor. This pole is an important part of the dance, as it is selected by the Holy Man, cut by the dancers and carried by them to the ceremony.

This pole is placed upright in the center of a large circular structure called an arbor that the dancers help build. It is a carefully selected straight tree shaped like a "Y" at the top. Cross beams, made from long, slender trees about thirty feet long, form the roof of the arbor. They are joined at the center pole. They place a nest of branches at the top of the pole for the eagle or thunderbird.

People make prayer wraps and tie many different colors of cloth around the center pole which is about a foot in diameter. When the ties are put in place on the pole, it becomes nearly three times as large in diameter, and as high as can be reached.

Before the dance, the dancers go through a purification ceremony in a sweat lodge built near the arbor. Then they are ready to begin the Thunder Dance. The arbor contains a fire circle for an eternal fire fed by a big log, an area for the singers and drum, and an enclosed resting place for the dancers.

Each time a song begins, the dancers come into the circle facing the center pole. An eagle-bone whistle hangs from a cord worn around their necks. They place the whistle between their teeth, hands at their sides, and all chant with the whistles simultaneously as they dance up and down in place with their faces lifted to the center pole. The Creator hears the whistles. The combined sound of the whistles, drum and singers can reach a high, uniform chant that uplifts our spirits.

Quills from porcupine, beads, painted designs, eagle fluffs, or feathers can adorn the whistles.

The dancers try to dance every song. If they miss one it makes the ceremony more difficult because the dancer loses his momentum. Their goal is to try to dance every time the singers and drum start, and go the full four days without food or water.

After the ceremony, the cloth is removed from the center pole, and anyone can go and pray at the pole.

Once when I went up to pray at the end of a Thunder Dance, there were hands all over the pole. When I finished my prayers and turned around to leave the arbor, I felt tears running down my face. Aunt Jenny, the medicine woman, was sitting outside the arbor. As I walked toward her, she smiled and told me that you could tell when a person's prayers were sincere by the tears shed. Outside there was a variety of blankets stacked in a mound about seven feet high. It consisted of star quilts, square patch quilts and Pendleton blankets. These were gifts to those who had journeyed to pray at the Thunder Dance.

Sometimes during the dance a thunder cloud appears over the sacred ceremony. I attended one during the middle of a drought and witnessed rain clouds moving toward us at the end of the fourth day.

POWWOW

Powwow is derived from the Algoguian word "pau wau." It means, "He dreams." Although today's powwows retain some religious significance, this isn't as pervasive as it was in earlier times.

The white man perceived Indian dancing as a threat until the late 1800s and early 1900s, particularly those performed by the fierce Plains Indians. They saw all Indian dances as "war dances" and prohibited them.

The reemergence of the powwow was related to the ceremonies instituted on reservations to honor the veterans returning home from the wars engaged in by the United States. These ceremonies caused a new-found Native American pride. By the end of World War II, the old ceremonies were revitalized. Tribes joined together for the first time in this new pride. This led to intertribal powwows in which dances, songs, and other observances were shared.

Today the many different types of powwows held throughout the country also include selling or trading arts and crafts, and feasting on traditional Native American foods. Dance, however, remains the highlight of the powwow.

Today's dances include Round Dances or Circle Dances, performed by facing the center of the powwow arena in a circle. Dancers circle left with various styles of footwork while keeping time with the drum.

Straight Dance is one of the oldest forms of Plains Indian dance, and involves straight posture while dancers primarily move up and down in fluid motion to the beat of the drum.

The Slide or Shuffle Dance is done to a double beat. Sometimes it is changed to a staggered beat and referred to as the Crow Hop, done by hopping to noticeably solid beats.

Soldier Dances were developed after World War I to honor

veterans. The beat is similar to the Round Dance, but is slower as time is kept to every other beat.

The Stomp Dance begins in a kneeling position as if scouting for an enemy, followed by a burst of dancing. Dancers move forward to symbolize non-retreating.

The Grass Dance is one of the oldest dances and still used in powwow. Religious in nature, it evolved from warrior society dances. It portrays a warrior in search of a proper ceremonial place. The dancer moves in imitation of tall swaying prairie grass.

Dreams or visions were the basis of the Jingle Dress Dance. The dress for this dance is fashioned with such items as small hawk bells, shells, or sewing thimbles to give it sound. The dance was originally used as medicine. Movements have undergone several transitions, and today dancers twist their feet in unison to the right and left while moving sideways.

The Fancy Shawl Dance, one of the most popular dances with women today, originated with middle-aged tribal women, and eventually spread to younger women. As it evolved, shawls were added. Today, the body and shawl are kept in harmony with the drum beat.

These and other dances can be seen at the hundreds of powwows held throughout the country. For a listing of dances see "Annual Powwow Events" listed in the appendix.

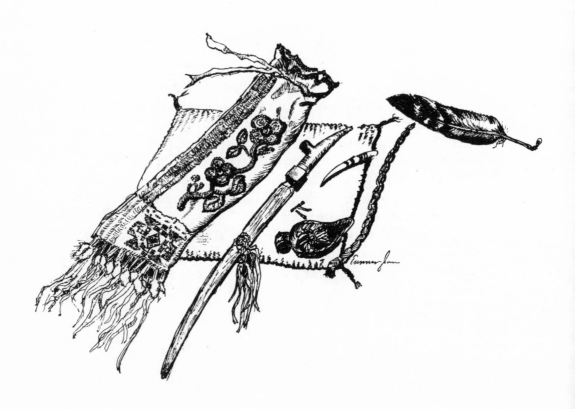

IV

OUR SACRED PIPES

▲

The pipe is used in most of our sacred ceremonies to call on spirit helpers and to send messages to the Creator. Mainly we call them "sacred pipes" or "ceremonial pipes."

My sacred pipe is more than 150 years old. The last time it was used before I received it appears to be in the late 1800s. The medicine person who last used it didn't finish his ceremony, because the tobacco left in the bowl was half burned. I removed the tobacco during cleaning and saved it for a medicine bag. The tobacco was cut in the old way, in small squares. A medicine person doesn't leave tobacco in a pipe after ceremony. Possibly he was killed by attackers before he completed the ceremony.

I came by the pipe through a friend, Leonard Wheatley. Leonard is a master leather worker who made rawhide drum heads for Native Americans, tack for horses, and bullwhips for entertainers and stuntmen. He couldn't ignore my attraction to the pipe, so finally he gave it to me. I had no idea at the time that it would help lead me to my spiritual path, or that I was to become a pipe keeper.

Although each medicine person differs in his or her medicine ways, one thing most medicine people of the Plains seem to agree on is that we take only tobacco as payment for conducting ceremonies. It doesn't matter what kind or how much tobacco—a pinch or a handful. All tobacco is sacred and any will do, even a cigarette. We don't consume the tobacco offering for pleasure. All is burned as offering to the Creator.

I've seen groups of people doing Native American ritual and asking for sums of money, medicine gifts (trinkets), or particular brands of cigarettes as offerings. It seems to me the Creator doesn't use money, need medicine gifts, nor smoke a certain brand of cigarettes.

I feel it's okay to gather goods, however, such as food and clothing for the needy people when we assemble together to pray at a ceremony or powwow. Participants at one of my seminars donated a truck load of staples to the Southern California Indian Center and distributed food to the needy. That is a different type of giving than the tobacco offering.

My pipe is very sacred to me, and used in ceremony for many purposes. The sacred pipe is a portable altar and the flesh of the people. Before I received my pipe, though, I prayed without it and the Creator still answered my prayers. Although the Creator hears and answers our prayers when we are alone, I believe that when we pray with the pipe in a group, our unified prayers are stronger. The pipe, therefore, has added another dimension to my life and I hope to the lives of others whenever we gather together in a ritual pipe ceremony. My pipe goes anywhere and everywhere, even into prisons. Although some medicine people don't believe the sacred pipe should be taken into a prison, it's really up to the individual keeper of each pipe. I believe it belongs wherever any human being needs help.

I have found that just because a person is in possession of a sacred pipe, doesn't mean they know how to use it in a Native American way. Nor is everyone who uses one a medicine person. Yet everyone is entitled to his or her own medicine. Only a person who has received directions from a Holy Man in the Native American tradition is allowed to do ceremony for others. Individuals, though, can gather together in prayer with personal sacred pipes.

Some pipes are personal or family pipes, and others can be

used in group ceremonies. There are no written instructions that come with the sacred pipe—just an old and ancient way of handling it that each tribe or medicine person follows and passes down orally. Our pipes vary in shape and size and each has a story.

Though I'm in possession of a sacred pipe, I do not consider it mine to own. It belongs to the people and is connected to all other sacred pipes. It is only taken from my pipe bag for ceremony after a tobacco offering, then used in a positive way.

To begin a ceremony, we smudge for purification purposes and then connect the two parts of the pipe—the bowl and the stem. This joining calls in the Creator and the grandfathers to listen to our prayers. We disconnect the pipe when the ceremony is over. The bowl and stem are then wrapped separately and put away until the next ceremony. The only time I take out the pipe, other than ceremony, is for cleaning or repair. Even at this time, I perform the standard rituals, such as smudging before I touch the pipe.

It's very disturbing for Native Americans to see the sacred pipes with the bowls and stems joined on display in museums or as decorations in homes. Those pipes are calling the Creator, and after a while the Creator and the grandfathers ignore these false calls. Then the pipe becomes invalid for praying and needs purification by a Holy Man before it is ever again used in ceremony.

Thus most Native Americans believe that sacred pipes do not belong in museums, but rather to their respective tribes and in the hands of medicine people who know how to care for them. Many Native Americans hope laws similar to the one passed in 1989 that requires returning identified Native American remains to their tribes, will be passed for other sacred artifacts such as the ceremonial pipes. The Smithsonian Institution became one of the first to return some remains to the Sioux Indians who sued under this new law.

PIPE BOWLS AND STEMS

The bowl of my pipe is made from catlinite, a sacred stone. Most catlinite pipestone in the United States comes from the western slope of a divide between the Mississippi and Missouri drainage on the north-central plains next to Pipestone Creek in Minnesota. Although this land fell into government hands, an 1858 treaty granted Indians the right to mine for pipestone. The area eventually became a national monument after years of court battles involving the rights of Native Americans versus white settlers. It is considered a sacred place by Native Americans today.

Pipestone is sometimes called "catlinite" for George Catlin, a 19th century artist who devoted his life to capturing the beauty of the American Indian on canvas and sketch. It's believed that he was the first white man to visit the pipestone quarries. A piece of the pipestone rests in the Washington Monument. Native Americans, though, prefer the term, "pipestone." A few Native American families today carry on the tradition of making the sacred pipes.

The red of the stone is referred to as, "The blood of the people," "Of the people," or "Flesh of the people." Some say it is also "Of the buffalo," because the buffalo played such an important part in the lives of Plains Indians.

Royal B. Hassrich writes about one story behind the red color of the pipestone in the *George Catlin Book of the American Indians*: "One of the myths describes a great flood. Thousands of Indians sought refuge on the heights of the quarry, but the waters rose and drowned them. The rocks of the quarry were stained red from the flesh of the bodies. And because of this, it became a holy place for all nations."

Barbara A. Hail, writing in *Hau, Kola!*, states that George Catlin was told by a Dakota Indian who lived near the pipestone quarry in Minnesota: "Many ages after the red men were made, when all the different tribes were at war, the Great Spirit sent runners and called them all together at the 'Red Pipe'. He stood on the top of the rocks, and the red people were assembled in infinite numbers on the plains below. He took out of the rock a piece of the red stone and made a large pipe. He smoked it over them all; told them that it was part of their flesh. He said that though they were at war they must meet at this place as friends, that it belonged to them all. The Great Spirit said that they must make their calumets from it and smoke them to him whenever they wished to appease him or get his goodwill. The smoke from his big pipe rolled over them all, and he disappeared in its cloud. At the last whiff of his pipe, a blaze of fire rolled over the rocks and melted their surface. At that moment, two squaws went in a blaze of fire under the two medicine rocks, where they remain to this day and must be consulted and propitiated whenever the pipe stone is to be taken away.''

Ceremonial pipes also are made of other natural stones and materials: clay, antler, rolled bark, steatite (soapstone), argillite (hardened mudstone), limestone and shale. Occasionally, pipes are made of metal, wood, or pottery. A caution for smoking a pipe of soapstone: soapstone contains the toxic and dangerouse substance, asbestos.

Stems usually are made of wood with a soft core such as sumac, oak or ash. Most Plains Indians prefer this kind of wood. Some stems are elaborately carved and hard woods are also sometimes used. Some stems are round and others flat. Plains Indians preferred round stems. My pipestem is round and made from white ash.

Branches are cut for the stems in the fall season when the sap is low. Pipe makers push a hot metal wire through the center of the stem when it is soft, or they can split a branch and scoop out the center pulp. The old method for joining the split pipe stem was to join the two halves with glue made from buffalo hooves, and to bind it with sinew. French Jesuits called the stems wands or reeds.

Sometimes only the stem was used in ceremony by Cree and other Plains Indians. The Mandans sometimes used a dried bird head and neck instead of a pipe bowl.

Most ceremonial pipe bowls are straight and smooth without carved effigies or symbols. The stem, though, was often highly decorated with eagle feathers, sweet grass, ribbons, beads, animal parts, leather, and fringe. Some stems were two inches across and three feet long. Most stems were shorter, between 18 inches and two feet. Shorter stemmed personal pipes with small bowls frequently were taken on hunting expeditions and war parties.

Many pipe bowls found in museums today are more ornate than those once used in ceremony. Some of the more ornate pipes were made by the Cherokee and by some non-Indians in the 1800s.

Plains Cree, Blackfoot and Plains Ojibwa generally have a specifically styled pipe called a micmac (from the Micmac Indian grouping in Canada and Newfoundland, with an Algonquian language heritage). The Micmac is shaped like a smoke stack from an old train. Other pipes used in ceremony by the majority of Plains Indians, including the Cree and Sioux, were T-shaped and elbow types. The T-shaped pipe was used by a family man, medicine person or Holy Man. The L-shaped pipe was usually smoked by bachelors (men without children) and women, whether or not they had children.

Most ceremonial pipes have no carving on them, yet fancy ones can be used in ceremony. This includes the effigy, which depicts carved animals, people or birds. The Cherokee were noted for making pipes with erotic carvings.

An early type pipe once used by many Native Americans is the disk, characterized by a small hole within a bowl shaped like a small saucer.

Clay pipes are popular with Southwest Indians. The Navajos use a clay pipe for healing. These pipes are made with a large bowl and short stem, coated with pine pitch. They smoke them whenever they want to offer prayers for someone who is very sick. It also is used as a ceremonial pipe by medicine men and women of the tribe.

PIPE HISTORY

In the early days, the pipe was lit from a burning coal that was packed in a horn container to be carried to the ceremony. Later Native Americans began using flint and steel brought by the Europeans. It became the standard way to light the pipes.

The earliest pipes were simple one-piece tubes, usually made of bone or stone. Some stone pipes and the later pipe-stone or catlinite pipes incorporated separate wooden stems.

The term "peace pipe" is rarely used by Native Americans and was coined by non-Indians when the white man began negotiating for land. It's also a spinoff from the way we used to "sign" our contracts with other tribes. In trading we would lay a pipe between the two parties and pile the exchange goods on each side of it.

Some ceremonial pipes, known as calumets, were believed to have contained very sacred power. Sometimes the pipes were made in pairs and used when warring tribes made peace treaties. The name, calumet, is from a Norman-French word meaning "reed" or "tube."

Anytime the catlinite pipe is smoked for ceremonial purposes or for personal use, it is still considered the sacred stone. I smoke a pleasure pipe made of briar and wouldn't think of using it for ceremonial purposes.

Primitive Plains Indians usually didn't smoke a pipe in a casual way. It was a shared experience with other men (sometimes women) to generate conversation, settle disputes and work out problems, or for success in hunting and war. It also was used to call to the spiritual powers of creation—meaning the bear, eagle, lion, wolf, or others.

Young warriors were sometimes discouraged from smoking a pipe except for ceremonial purposes because the Indian realized it was bad for their health and stamina. Still, smoking wasn't considered as harmful then as it is today. Tobacco was used in moderation. It was natural and was not laced with chemicals like modern cigarettes.

During tribal ceremonies, the ashes from the pipe were usually deposited in special places by the altar or around the lodge where it was smoked or used as medicine for physical or spiritual healing. Great care was given to the placement of the ashes. Sometimes the medicine person gave it to someone in need of medicine. Today, I usually give the ashes to the person asking for the ceremony or to someone who needs medicine.

PIPE TRADITIONS

Sacred pipes were given to tribes in different ways by the Great Spirit. These tribes have their own traditions. For example, the Lakota, who comprise the seven tribes of the Western Sioux, originally were given the pipe by the White Buffalo Calf Woman. In their legend, one of the two men who met the White Buffalo Calf Woman was killed because of his lusting after her. The other man returned to the tribe and told them to prepare for a visit from the White Buffalo Calf Woman. She then came to them and gave instructions for the pipe's use. It's said that the original pipe is still preserved by the Lakota.

The Dakota (the eastern Sioux) tribes' tradition, says that a maiden dressed in white buckskin approached the two men. The one who lusted after her was killed and the other brought the pipe she was carrying to his tribe. He was made the pipe holder.

Some traditions say that the sacred pipe existed before the creation of animals and land. Others link the pipe to a spirit-person responsible for thunder.

A Blackfoot tale says that Thunder revealed an original pipe after a tribesman's daughter did a favor for a bear. Robert H. Lowie writes in *Indians of the Plains* that such a pipe is on display at the American Museum of Natural History. Blackfeet, who are noted for their spectacular pipes, sometimes call them "thunder's pipes."

Some attribute spiritual happenings, or what might be termed "supernatural" or "magical" powers, to our pipe ceremonies. Mystery can be all sacred and so can knowledge. When you understand the unknown, it is still sacred but with new meaning. What can be wrong with still seeing a man in the moon, or envisioning thunder beings in the storm clouds? Awe, humbleness, and mystery bring us closer to the universe or the power of the Creater.

This power is real to us. For example: many medicine people don't wear watches, jewelry, belt buckles, or other metal objects when conducting ceremonies because it is believed that metal could be burned into our flesh by the energy force that sometimes visits us during ceremony.

PIPE BAGS

After using the pipe, the parts are disconnected, cleaned, wrapped in separate red cotton cloth, and placed in a parflech (a rawhide container, such as a box, envelope or pouch) or a special pipe bag. Some of these bags are made of brain-tanned deer skin, elk or buffalo, as well as canvas, cotton or wool. Some tribes decorated these parfleches elaborately.

My pipe bag is made from brain-tanned deer skin and smoked to keep the tanning process from going out of the leather. Brain-tanning is an old Native American process using the brains, heart and liver of the animal to tan the hide. No chemicals are added.

We decorate most pipe bags with such things as beads, porcupine quills, tin cones (decorative tin) and small hawk bells. They are also painted with natural substances for color.

My pipe bag is decorated with Woodland, Plains Cree and Metis bead design of several colors with fringe and tin cones at the bottom. Horsehair sticks out of the cones. The top opening is scalloped and beaded. The bag also shows a thunderbird made in small, blue cobalt beads. Flowers, small birds and geometrical Cree designs are on both sides.

A non-Indian and special friend, Jim, who does fine beadwork, beaded the bag for me. I asked him to smudge with sage before working on it, and according to Native American custom, to leave it alone when his wife was in her moon. He did this and, when the bag was complete, said that it was about the best bead work he had ever done.

Pipe containers aren't sacred to me, but we put sacred objects in them. I look at our bags and parfleches as protection for sacred objects. Yet, they can also be objects of beauty because Native Americans like to be surrounded by beauty and creation.

Other things put in pipe bags include our ceremonial blend of tobacco, sage, cedar, sweet grass and pipe tamper, smudge-burning container, kitchen matches, and feathers.

We use the sacred pipe wherever and whenever the need for prayers arises. The Creator and the grandfathers observe us wherever we are. Anywhere we gather with pipe and prayer is our church—in Thunder Dance, vision quest, sweat lodge, a house, a field, the mountains or plains, in a basement or around a campfire.

PIPE SMOKING SUBSTANCES

To my knowledge, medicine people don't use drugs in the sacred pipe ceremony. Nor am I aware of its use by Native American medicine people at any time during the history of the sacred catlinite pipestone era. There is a history, however, and great misconceptions about the Native American use of hallucinogens.

Jimson weed (Datura) was used by some Plains Indians during male initiation rites and vision quests, but was not used in the sacred pipes. Also, Jimson weed wasn't smoked.

Some Native Americans in the northeast smoked a tobacco substitute, the cardinal flower, which is an herbal medicine. The plant, which can have drug-like side effects, erroneously became known as "Indian tobacco" by settlers.

Peyote cults were first reported in the sixteenth century in South America and from there traveled north through the North American continent to Canada by the twentieth century. Peyote was then used in Native American ceremony and ritual as medicine and for visions involving upcoming battles.

Today it is used mostly by a fractional number of Native Americans and as a focus of the Native American Church, which is an organized Peyote religion. The church is estimated to have more than 200,000 members. It is a combination of Christianity and Native Americanism with many rituals from the Native American culture. Peyote can legally be used within the confines of the church's ceremonies and rituals.

Native Americans use ceremonial mixes of tobacco and herbs in their pipes according to the tradition of their tribe, or from a vision by the Holy Man. Most common ceremonial tobacco is composed of bearberry and red willow bark. Additives include red sumac, sage, twist tobacco and other herbs. Sometimes berry juice is added to the mix in remembrance of the thunderbird and eagle who eat the berries in the spring.

PASSING THE PIPE

If you're in a pipe ceremony and are unfamiliar with it, pay attention to how the pipe is passed. Handle the pipe the way the one before you (the person to your right) does. Try not to sit right next to the pipe keeper so you can watch the way he handles the pipe. Medicine people light the pipe with matches in most ceremonies, but in the sweat lodge we sometimes light it with sweet grass. *Hold the pipe bowl in your left hand, the stem in your right hand. Take four puffs. Blow the smoke to the Creator. Do not point the stem or spin the pipe. Just smoke it without inhaling it and pass it on.* If you don't smoke because of age or health reasons, touch the stem to your right shoulder, then to the left shoulder and pass it to the left, handing it to the next person. This also applies to children.

In the fall of 1985, I went to Santa Monica, California for a meeting of the Big Mountain Support Group concerned with preserving the Hopi/Navajo land that overlaps portions of Colorado, New Mexico, Arizona and Utah. The government and other interested parties were (and still are) trying to take it away. A few medicine people were invited to attend, including John Funmaker. After the meeting, I was asked to do a pipe ceremony. There were about twenty-eight men gathered in the circle. Since I had recently returned from the reservation in Montana where I had been given directions, my pipe felt very strong.

I was told by the Holy Man in Montana that women shouldn't be in the sacred pipe ceremony. In Santa Monica, after doing my directions with the pipe and loading it, a woman stepped into the circle. She was a Japanese Buddhist nun. She wore a colorful robe of brown, white, and orange. Her hood slipped and I noticed her head was shaven. She carried a hand drum used for chanting. I continued to light the pipe and

passed it around. When it reached her, she was very respect-
ful of the pipe and seemed to know how to handle it. The pipe
went around the circle and back to me without going out,
which is very unusual with that many people participating. I
found out later that the woman had smoked often with many
Holy Men and medicine people's sacred pipes. I later also realized from this experience that people from many different
faiths have an interest in Native American tradition. By taking part in other ceremonies and ways, they enrich their own
spiritual paths.

Although the tradition has been that only men smoke the
sacred pipe on some reservations and that women have their
own ceremonies, ways have changed to adapt to modern-day
people and times. Although we live in a different world today
than that of our ancestors, reverence for the earth and respect
for our Creator, ancestors, families and friends need never
change.

V

MOTHER EARTH CEREMONIALS, MEDICINES AND FOODS

▲

CEREMONIAL BLENDS

Tobacco (Kinnikinnick) is sacred and is used for almost all offerings. In the old days some tribes had tobacco societies which were in charge of tobacco growing. Although most of the time it was used during ceremony, tobacco was also used at designated times for pleasure.

My ceremonial mix has native tobacco, bearberry (larve, which it the native term), sage, a black tobacco, and some berry-flavored tobacco (because the thunderbird and the eagle eat berries).

I believe in honoring some of the other ceremonial blends used by other tribes. Sometimes I put red willow bark and red sumac in the mix. The Lakota used red willow bark ceremonially to make their kinnikinnick. I like the smell of the smoke from the red willow.

Some ingredients for the pipe also serve as medicines. A poultice made of some tobacco can be used to stop bleeding. Some Native American tribes used tobacco to cure earache by blowing in the ears of those infected. Native Americans used bearberry as medicine to promote the flow of urine, to strengthen the bladder and kidneys, and to treat female disorders.

When a pipe is used in ceremony, the smoke is not inhaled because it is very strong. It isn't the same as a pleasure smoke from an ordinary pipe. Its purpose is to carry our prayers to the Creator.

Because we consider tobacco sacred, we leave it for the Creator and grandmother earth in offering when we gather herbs and sage. We also use tobacco in prayer ties and offerings for sick people.

Sage is one of our most widely used herbs for smudges. It is originally from Southern Europe, introduced to North America about 300 years ago. Although we use the leaves, the stem makes a good pipe tamper or cleaner. It makes no difference which type of sage you use. Many use sage brush because it is so plentiful in many areas. The herb sage (not brush) is more difficult to find. June and July are the best times to gather most types of sage, but blue sage in best in August. Sage usually grows in rocky areas. I prefer the sage from the Northern plains and I also use California sage, which seems more pungent. Some sage is stronger smelling while other kinds have a very light aroma.

Sage is well-known as a seasoning for cooking and as a winter foliage food for livestock. It's also used in teas, medicine, and as an oil. Some Native Americans place dried sage over windows and doors to purify the home and all who come and go.

Lower California Native Americans used sage in several ways. They ground the seeds and stirred them in water as a beverage to prevent evaporation in the mouth and throat according to Virgil J. Vogel in *American Indian Medicine*.

In *Earth Medicine, Earth Food*, author Michael A. Weiner, writes: "California sage (various Salvia species) was used by Native American healers. Wild sage (Salvia lyrata) was employed by the Catawbas, on the east coast. The roots were pounded into a salve and applied to sores. 'Salvia officinalis' was entered in the U.S. Pharmacopoeia from 1842 to 1916, where it was recommended for its tonic, astringent, and aromatic properties, given in dyspepsia [indigestion]."

When gathering sage, try to find a clean area away from traffic and pollutants. Sage grows everywhere and can even be found in a vacant city lot. It may seem more spiritual to go out in the country or mountains to gather it, but not all people have that option.

After you have picked the sage, offer a small amount of tobacco as a way of thanking grandmother earth for the sage she has provided. One leaves tobacco offerings in his or her own way, whether throwing it in one spot or scattering it around the circle of your harvest area.

Take only the amount of sage that you need and maybe a little more for a friend. Don't pick an area clean. Take small amounts from separate clusters. Walk around and enjoy the outdoors because gathering sage is itself a sacred act or ceremony. Try to leave no trace of yourself when you gather sage and other herbs or medicine.

Once gathered, sage can be wrapped with thread in a small bundle before drying. This keeps the leaves from shedding and provides a torch-like bundle that is handy for smudging.

Some people dry sage in the direct sun, others pick an area for drying that gets the morning sun and the afternoon shade. You can also put it in the shade for slow drying. I wouldn't recommend drying it in an oven because I feel it works better if it is sun dried. I try to use a natural and traditional way of drying.

Many reservation Native Americans store the sage in an empty bread wrapper, or a cotton, canvas or leather bag. Any storage container is acceptable.

Most Native Americans use the type of sage that grows in their area. Most regions contain two or three standard types of sage and each type may be used for different purposes. Some types are used around the house to keep a balance of energy. Another type of sage may be used by medicine people. Still, another sage will be used in personal prayers. People have a sense for what is pleasing to them and what works.

Sage can be used for blessing your flower or vegetable garden. Before turning the soil, smudge yourself with sage and then smudge the land, the plants, and seeds to be offered to grandmother earth. Ask the Creator to bless your labors. Then, make a small tobacco offering and pray. Smudge yourself whenever you go out to work in your garden. This process will help you maintain balance with nature. When the plants are ready for harvesting, repeat the smudging. Offer tobacco to mother earth and a prayer.

Cedar helps remove negative spirits from your circle of prayer when sage isn't enough. It removes bad feelings from objects such as personal belongings and places like houses, business areas, and gathering places. It can also be used in mourning.

Sometimes I use cedar, sage and sweet grass to smudge a house. The cedar pushes out bad feelings and spirits. We use it in the sweat lodge on the sacred rocks.

In smudging, use the dark green leaves of the cedar tree and not the wood shavings. Some foliage in the clusters are round. Other are flat. I use both, but prefer the round because it seems to smell better. When harvesting cedar, again leave a tobacco offering.

The wood from the cedar can be used as a natural deterrent for moths and other bugs that will eat feathers, wool and natural fiber clothes.

Sometimes we are drawn to areas and things that have special energy and meaning for us. While I was gathering cedar one day, I noticed a tree which had been struck by lightning.

I gathered cedar from that tree because I believed the medicine was stronger since the thunder beings had put their energy into the tree.

Sweet grass is used to bring in the good spirits, as they like the sweet smell. The negative spirits do not like the honey-like aroma. Through visions and dreams, our medicine people have told us the way in which to use sweet grass.

Sweet grass grows only in certain areas of the Northern Plains. It grows in medium to dark green clusters to heights of about two feet. During droughts it can be difficult to find.

We use sweet grass in some of our healing and pipe ceremonies, sweat lodges, sun dances, thunder dances, and vision quests. It is commonly used in Plains' ceremony. During healing ceremonies sometimes a sick person is touched with a braid of sweet grass as part of the rituals. It is also used by Native Americans to make baskets.

Medicine men often keep sweet grass in their medicine bags with other roots and herbs. They touch the sweet grass to the hot sacred rocks in the sweat lodge to light the sacred pipes. Sometimes, medicine people will tie a braid of sweet grass to the stems of their pipes.

I like to have a braid of sweet grass lying on my altar when performing a pipe ceremony for the good spirits and feelings it brings to the circle.

Sweet grass smells sweeter than fresh cut lawn grass. When burning, it smells like fragrant, sugared smoke.

You can sometimes buy sweet grass at shops that carry Native American supplies or at powwows. Sweet grass usually comes braided, tied at the bottom with a blade of the grass, and looped into a knot at the top.

HERBS

Native Americans believe that herbs are our brothers and sisters. Herbs have nutrients and energies that feed and nuture us. This, in turn, helps our bodies to heal themselves.

The white man once scoffed at Native American medicine. Today the United States Pharmacopoeia lists more than 200 drug-yielding herbs or plants derived from Native American culture. There are many more used by tribal healers, medicine people, and women of the tribe.

The remedies my grandmother used on me when I was sick were of Native American origin. She made a heated mixture of cayenne, ginger, sugar, and whiskey to settle upset stomaches.

Loren Nelson, who with his father, Lee Nelson, cofounded the American Indian Herb Company in San Diego, California, contributed the following information on herbs. This material came from his research for a forthcoming book on herbs that will include those used by Native Americans. Loren maintains a full-time holistic health practice and travels throughout the country teaching and lecturing on herbs, nutrition, acupuncture, acupressure, meditation, graphology and body movement efficiency.

Since herbs grow in abundance all over the earth, those in a person's particular area usually will be adequate to complete a good medicine bag. Medicine men and women usually gather all they need from their local area. Approximately thirty herbs can serve as the basis for general healings.

Herbs fall into different categories determined by their site of action, attraction to a specific area of the body, or when mixed. The pharmacological effects of an herbal combination are difficult to analyze because the formula may consist of four to twelve individual herbs interacting with one another.

Three types of interactions occur with herbs: 1. between individual herbs; 2. between the constituents of individual herbs; and 3. between the constituents of different herbs.

The pharmacological effects of herbal combinations on the body prove complex. Interactions involve: 1. SYNERGISM which occurs when two constituents that are mixed multiply, or enhance the pharmacological actions; 2. ANTAGONISM that occurs when two constituents are mixed creating either a competitive or noncompetitive effect and; 3. TRANSITION that occurs when two or more herbs change the action or effect of individual herbs.

There exist seven possible effects from the previously mentioned interactions. They are:

1. Single effect: A formula containing only one herb possesses one therapeutic effect.

2. Additive effect: Two or more kinds of herbs with similar properties used in combination can mutually reinforce the therapeutic actions.

3. Synergic effect: Two or more ingredients cause one to act as the principal substance while the rest play subsidiary roles, thus reinforcing the action of the principal ingredient.

4. Mutual restraint or antagonistic effect: Two or more ingredients in a prescription can weaken or neutralize each other's action.

5. Counteraction or inhibitive effect: The action of one herb may inhibit the action of another.

6. Destructive or neutralizing effect: One herb or ingredient neutralizes the toxicity of another one.

7. Incompatible or opposite effect: When two herbs produce toxicity and drastic side effects.

There are several methods of herb processing aimed at reducing toxicity, removing adverse effects, promoting therapeutic effects, altering herb properties, and cleansing and removing odors.

Herbs are purified after harvesting through a water process, either by washing, immersing, moistening, leaching, water-

screening, or soaking. This process also makes them soft and easy to cut. Some herbs require special additives to remove toxicity, so extreme care and knowledge are needed.

Other methods of purifying herbs involve fire processings such as stir-frying, sand-heating, wrapped roasting, flame-heating, ash-heating and baking. Water-fire processing involves steaming, cooking, tempering (dropping in vinegar to make brittle after heating), boil-scalding, or stewing. Herbs can also be defatted or ashed by compression and then strained to remove the oil content. They can be blended or fermented to purify.

Once processed, herbs are available in the following twenty forms:

1. Slices
2. Pills
3. Powder
4. Plaster
5. Tan
6. Medicated liquor
7. Herbal distillate
8. Pellets
9. Glue formed into small cubes or bars
10. Tea
11. Tablets
12. Capsules
13. Tincture
14. Fluid extract
15. Instant granules
16. Ointment
17. Syrups
18. Suppositories
19. Aerosols
20. Injections

Here is a list of plants and what they treat:

BLOOD SYSTEM
Golden Seal
Echinacea

Yellow Dock
Capsicum
Red Clover
Wild Cherry Bark

LIVER
Red Root
Poplar
Parsley
Dandelion
Celery Seed
Tamarack

KIDNEY
Dandelion
Juniper Berries

URINARY TRACT
Juniper Berries
Poplar
Irish Moss
DIURETICS
Buchu Lus
Horsetail Grass
Irich Moss
Dandelion

LUNGS
Yarrow
Mullein
Wild Cherry Bark
Yerba Santa
Marshmallow

NERVOUS SYSTEM
Valerian Root
Mistletoe
Lobelia

PAIN SUPPRESSANTS
Catnip
Black Willow
Blue Violet

STOMACH-INTESTINES
Chamomile
Fennel
Slippery Elm
All Mints

MENSTRUAL DYSFUNCTION
Mugworth
Myrtle
Penny Royal

PENETRATORS
Yucca
Tamarack
Mullein

WORMING
Wormwood
Motherwort
Aloes
Catnip
Celery

Plants and herbs containing the following minerals are listed in order of potency for each grouping.

CALCIUM
    Sesame seed (whole)
    Kelp
    Irish moss
    Dulse
    Parsley
    Dandelion
    Orange peel
    Watercress
    Capsicum
    Fennel
    Dock
    Carrot

PHOSPHORUS
    Sesame seed (whole)
    Dulse
    Capsicum
    Kelp
    Irish moss
    Dandelion
    Parsley
    Watercress
    Fennel
    Dock
    Carrot
    Plantain
    Orange peel
    Chicory

Papaya
Caraway
Chickweed
Marigold flowers
Licorice root

IRON
Dulse
Kelp
Sesame seed (whole)
Irish moss
Capsicum
Parsley
Dandelion leaves
Fennel
Watercress
Yellow Dock
Orange peel
Plantain
Carrot
Chicory
Papaya
Nettle
Burdock
Mullein leaves

IODINE
Kelp
Dulse
Carrot
Grapefruit peel
Irish moss
Sarsaparilla

SODIUM
Kelp
Irish moss
Dulse
Capsicum
Dandelion
Sesame seed (whole)
Watercress
Carrot
Parsley
Chicory
Dock
Black willow bark
Orange peel
Papaya
Grapefruit peel
Mistletoe
Nettle
Raspberry leaves
Alfalfa

POTASSIUM
Dulse
Kelp
Irish moss
Capsicum
Parsley
Sesame seed (whole)
Dandelion
Fennel
Dock
Watercress
Papaya

Orange peel
Chicory
Grapefruit peel
Mistletoe
Chamomile
Alfalfa
Comfrey
Peppermint

MAGNESIUM
Kelp
Dulse
Sesame seed (whole)
Parsley
Dandelion
Carrot
Watercress
Chicory
Grapefruit peel
Alfalfa
Black willow
Mistletoe
Mullein

COPPER
Alfalfa
Cabbage
Spinach
Almonds
Dried beans

SULPHUR
Watercress
Dock

Kelp
Carrot
Dandelion
Chicory
Orange peel
Grapefruit peel
Mullein

ZINC
Sarsaparilla
Kelp
Dandelion
Citrus
Green vegetables
Dates
Most fish
Beets
Banana
Wheat germ
Molasses
Egg yolk

MANGANESE
Black walnuts
Parsley
Beets
Lettuce
Alfalfa
Spinach

CHLORINE
Kelp
Dock
Watercress

Dandelion
Carrot
Chicory
Grapefruit peel
Orange peel
All plants, more or less

FLUORINE
Watercress
Beets
Garlic
Spinach

SILICON
Dandelion leaves
Horsetail grass
Oat straw
Iceberg lettuce
Spinach
Carrot
Orange peel

For more information refer to the Bibliography under Herbs.

FOODS

Native Americans make use of about 1,500 indigenous plants as food staples. The original food of the Plains Indians consisted of meat, fish, berries, acorns and other nuts, roots, wild rice and fruits. They also ate maple sugar, maize, beans and squashes. More than one thousand wild foods are still available today.

Native Americans existed on a high fat diet that would be unacceptable by today's standards, but was necessary for the vigorous and hard life they led. An example of this diet is pemmican, a dried meat (usually buffalo) stored for the winter. It was dried, pounded and mixed with a variety of wild berries or choke cherries (with pits). Lard was heated and mixed throughout the pemmican serving as a natural preservative and providing the fat needed to sustain energy during the winter months. It was put into a buffalo hide and sometimes buried in a cache for future use. A recent dig revealed a partially edible store of this meat supply buried in the early 1800s. Early Mountain Men learned this process from the Native Americans.

Buffalo, elk, deer, and moose provided the main meat source for Plains Indians. Woodland bands used deer, elk, and other smaller animals and salmon for their main meats. Maize was a staple of many tribes, but others preferred the wild rice that grew abundantly in many areas. Nuts such as acorn, hickory, chestnut and butternut were as important to the diet as fruit. The inner bark of the hemlock tree provided fiber and nutrients when made into dried cakes.

Because Native Americans lived closely with their food sources and existed on a delicate balance with nature, they were very thankful for their food.

When I was very young, my grandmother made a mixture of ground meat, rice, and raisins periodically and served it for dinner. I learned as an adult that the mixture is used as a food offering to help Indians remember the times of hunger.

As an infant, I was breast fed and later found I was allergic to cow's milk, as are many Native American children.

Before we ate any meal with Aunt Jenny Gray, the medicine woman, she would pick up every food container from the table, even a cereal box, and say a prayer for each.

Many dishes prepared today by Native Americans are only reflections of their previous diets since it would be all but impossible to live off the land as they once did.

The following recipes are based on Native American cooking but done in a modern way.

Beef Jerky (Dried Meat)

This jerky is made by cutting a brisket or shank portion of beef into thin strips while it is still slightly frozen for easier cutting. The strips are soaked in a beef marinade, such as Teriyaki, overnight.

Before drying, black pepper, red peppers or other flavorings can be added to portions of the marinated meat. The strips are placed directly on the racks of a gas oven and baked below 100 degrees for 8–12 hours (allow for altitude).

(Contributed by Jenny Busby)

Native Americans make different types and shapes of fry bread. It is a non-baked, non-yeast bread often used like a thick tortilla. In the Northern Plains, they shape it like a rectangular donut. The Southwest Native Americans use the round pancake style. I prefer the rectangular shape because it's easier to handle while eating it plain. Round bread makes a great Navajo taco when meat, beans, lettuce, tomato and onions are placed on top. Other ways of fixing fry-bread are with powdered sugar, pie fillings or honey. Each fry-bread maker has his or her own secret recipe.

Fry-bread is quick and easy to make and found at most pow-wows. It is also served as a traditional snack at many other social gatherings. Traditional fry bread was made with lard, but many Native Americans are now using healthier types of oils. Here is just one of the many fry bread recipes:

Fry-Bread

4 cups flour, 3 tbls. baking powder, 1 tbl. salt,
2 tbls. margarine or lard, 2 cups water.

Blend the dry ingredients in a large bowl. Add water in the middle and knead with your hands. Flour your hands and pull off a ball of dough about the size of a golf ball. Place on a floured board and flatten. Roll with a floured rolling pin into a round circle about ¼ inch thick. Drop it into a skillet of about 1–2 inches of lard or cooking oil. Cook until lightly browned and bubbled. Drain on paper towels.

Some Native Americans add a small amount of sugar to the original dough mixture.

(Contributed by Fran Dancing Feather)

Rice Water: Horchata, rice water, is a pleasant and sweet drink.

1 cup uncooked rice, sugar or sweetener to taste,
cinnamon to taste and about 1 tbl. vanilla.

Place half the rice in a blender and fill with water to the top. Blend. Let sit for about 5 minutes, letting sediment settle to the bottom. Pour pour the top liquid into a container. Continue adding a little of the rice to what is already in the blender and add water for about four more blendings. Each blending should continue for about 5 minutes. After each sitting, pour top liquid into container. Add the sugar, cinnamon, and vanilla and refrigerate.

(Contributed by Fran Dancing Feather)

Corn Pudding

1 qt. milk, ⅓ cup cornmeal (white or yellow),
½ cup figs, dates or raisins, ½ tsp. cinnamon,
½ cup brown sugar, ½ tsp. salt, ½ tsp. ginger, 1 egg.

Place milk in double boiler, scald and add corn meal (you might have to moisten it with a little bit of cold water). Stir constantly to prevent lumping. When consistency is thick, slowly add the lightly beaten egg and blend. Cook 20 minutes on low heat. Place in casserole dish (oven proof). Add all other ingredients except egg. Stir vigorously. Place in oven set at 300 degrees and bake for 1 hr. Use favorite sauce over the pudding.

(Contributed by Dean Allen)

Bannock Bread: This is an easy stove-top bread still made today.
   2 cups flour, ¼ tsp. salt, 3 tsps. baking powder,
   ½ cup shortening, about ½ cup water.
Mix dry ingredients and cut in the shortening the same as for pie dough. Add the water and knead for about 10 minutes until the dough is smooth. Grease an iron skillet, press the dough into the pan and bake on top of the stove over very low heat. Free the bottom and sides of the pan when one side is browned and turn it over. Total cooking time is 15–20 minutes.

Berry Soup: This hearty dish is made with lean beef (or buffalo) and blackberries.
   1 pound lean beef, 2 tbls. vegetable oil,
   1 peeled and sliced medium onion,
   about 3 cups beef broth (can be canned),
   1 cup fresh or frozen blackberries, 1 tbl. light honey.
Broil the beef and cut into ½-inch squares. Brown the onions in the oil in a Dutch oven. Add the chunks of meat, blackberries, beef stock and honey. Cook about 1 hour, or until meat is tender.

Jerky Stew: This is a good dish to make and serve on a camping trip.

   1 lb. beef jerky, 1 large can hominy,

   1 large peeled and chopped onion,

   2 large unpeeled potatoes, black pepper to taste.

Place 1-inch pieces of the jerky, the onion, and drained hominy in a heavy skillet. Cover with water and simmer covered for about 2 hours (you may have to add more water). Add the diced potatoes and cook until they are tender. Season with pepper to taste.

VI

GOOD MEDICINE
DOESN'T COME IN BOTTLES

▲

Many Native Americans feel that if they are not on their path, they aren't truly healthy. Although we seek guidance and help, the central feature of our medicine rests with the individual. Our Native American "doctors" heal on the physical, mental, and spiritual levels. Thus, our doctors can see the whole picture and have been ahead of current scientific and medical thought. They have always practiced what the contemporary non-Indian calls "holistic health."

Although we use herbs and plant remedies, we know that good medicine is spiritual—and more encompassing than the simple treatment of the body. It involves one's connection to the universe and following one's path during their journey here on earth. If a person is not balanced or in tune with the spirits, ancestors, loved ones, and if they are cut off from visions and dreams, they are not considered healthy.

Fritjof Capra, physicist, speaks of the multiple causes of disease in his book, *The Turning Point*: "Machines function according to linear chains of cause and effect, and when they break down a single cause for the breakdown can usually be identified. In contrast, the functioning of organisms is guided by cyclical patterns of information flow known as feedback loops. When such a system breaks down, the breakdown is usually caused by multiple factors that may amplify each other through interdependent feedback loops. Which of these factors was the initial cause of the breakdown is often irrelevant.

This nonlinear interconnectedness of living organisms indicates that the conventional attempts of biomedical science to associate diseases with single causes are highly problematic."

Many Native Americans still use the traditional medicine: herbs, plants, certain natural drugs, animal parts, healing, sweat lodges, vision quests, dreams, smudging, and positive thinking, as well as modern medicine, to keep their bodies and spirits well.

Although we are all healers and responsible for our own well-being, we sometimes rely on friends and family to help in healing and seek help from medicine people.

Native Americans stay away from making medical decisions for others, or using our healing methods without permission from the one needing healing. We don't want to be responsible for that person's path either in a positive or negative way. When one person enters the life of another by making decisions for them, they become responsible for that person's path.

Medicine people, whose names vary from tribe to tribe, usually include Holy Men or Women who are ceremonial leaders and also healers. They can also be pipe keepers charged with the keeping of sacred pipes used for ceremonial purposes; medicine men or women who are primarily healers; or herbalists trained in herb and other medicines. Sometimes there is what non-Indians call a diagnostician who discerns the problem. There can also be the wife who tends the healing at home even though she isn't officially termed a "medicine woman". Women are considered equal when it comes to healing, and are highly respected. Medicine women of our tribes have great gifts and a special calling to healing. Native Americans usually don't use the term "shaman" since it is a white man's term and borrowed from the Siberian word for medicine man.

Several Native American medicine people have traveled throughout Europe and to the Soviet Union to teach the Native American way and to let them know of our customs that still exist. In Germany they have large Indian Clubs where participants dress as Indians and set up tepees. Many Native American artifacts were taken to Europe during the early days of America, and interest has grown from them.

Some medicine people follow their paths by taking their medicine ways into the prisons. Others seek out those in need on the city streets. And some keep their medicine on the Indian reservation. But it is very apparent to me that some of our traditions and holy ways are being corrupted by pseudo-medicine people out to make money from these sacred ways. Charging people for spiritual teachings that have always been free, in my opinion, is not good medicine—especially since the Creator is the guide behind all healing.

It also seems ironic that after centuries of trying to stamp out our medicine men and women, the National Institute of Mental Health now pays to train medicine men and women on some reservations.

Nature has provided medicine for all people. Knowing how to use it though is essential. Herbs and plants used wrongly can cause serious side effects and even kill people. For example, the dried roots of sarsaparilla, related to the ginseng family, are used in a flavored drink. Portions of the plant were used by Native Americans for different medicines. Yet it can be toxic to the liver if used incorrectly.

Plains Cree were famous for their medicines throughout the land. Early traders, as well as other Native American tribes, sought out their herbal and medicinal remedies and cures. They made more money from selling their medicines to other tribes and to the white man than from fur trading.

I use both the old ways and traditional medicine successfully. I go for a yearly medical checkup and take the most effective treatment for a particular ailment, whether it be herbs or cough syrup. But because Native Americans want as much awareness as possible, we try to avoid taking prescribed drugs or medication for pain unless it is absolutely necessary.

The outdoors is considered also to be a great healing source. The sun, grandmother earth, the wind, the sky, and nature, all serve to uplift our spirits and contribute to our well being.

SWEAT LODGE HEALING

The sweat lodge is one of our most sacred ceremonies. It is used to purify oneself in body and spirit in preparation for communication with the Creator.

When you go to a sweat lodge, it is customary to bring tobacco for the medicine person who is essential for a true sweat lodge. You'll also need a towel and bathing suit or covering for your body. Native American people are usually modest. They are there to pray and purify. Bad thoughts dirty the sweat lodge.

If you are attending a sweat lodge for the first time, listen and watch others to learn what is expected. When the medicine person is ready, enter the sweat lodge clockwise and single file by crawling in the opening on hands and knees. Bending over and walking in, or duck walking would be arrogant in the eyes of the Creator. As you crawl in the sweat lodge you can say, "all my relations," and repeat it when you leave. Give the tobacco to the medicine person at the beginning of the ceremony.

When everyone is inside the heated rocks are usually brought in with a pitchfork from the hot coals outside where they have been heating for a couple of hours. Someone will sprinkle the cedar as a blessing on the glowing rocks inside the lodge. The rocks are then moved around inside, often with deer antlers, and checked to make certain no ashes or dirt are on them.

If the sprinkled cedar catches fire, whoever is nearest blows out the flame. You want the smudge or smoke from the cedar to permeate the lodge and to remove bad spirits. When the first group of forty rocks to be used are placed in the hole, the flap is closed. The first round of four doors begins. That means there will be four groups of rocks brought in, one group each for the four stages of purification that will take place in the sweat lodge. Four songs are sung for each different stage.

It will become warm and then very hot, especially after water is thrown on the rocks. Some people experience claustrophobia. It is best to take in shallow breaths and not breathe deeply. When you regain your composure and the steam is all around you, try to sing with the group. Or, if it is too hot, put your head close to mother earth. The more humble and relaxed you become, the easier it will be. Put your body and spirit in the hands of the Creator.

In this ceremony accompanying our own breath is the breath of the sacred stone people, which is the steam rising from the water thrown on the rocks. These rocks are the oldest living creations in the world and remind us of our own beginnings.

When the first door (stage) is open, relax and remain in the sacred circle if you can. Ask the people in the sweat to give you support. Most medicine people who are conducting a sweat will try not to make it too hot for the weakest, nor too mild for the strongest.

If you absolutely can't handle the heat, ask the medicine person conducting the sweat to excuse you after the first round. You need give no reason. It is your choice. After being excused, leave by going clockwise. Be careful not to touch or crawl across the hot rocks.

After the third round, the sacred pipe is sometimes brought in to help send our prayers to the Creator. This is the time to pay attention to how the pipe is passed around, and to handle it in the same way as the person to your right. The pipe will be lit with burning sweet grass, which was, in turn, lit from the hot rocks for the last door of the sweat. *Hold the pipe bowl in your left hand, the stem in your right hand. Take four puffs but do not inhale. Blow the smoke to the Creator. Do not point the stem or spin the pipe.* If you don't smoke because of personal reasons, touch the stem to your right shoulder and then to your left shoulder. Pass it to the left, handing it to the next person.

Try to follow what the others are doing. During one of the doors (stages), usually the third, drinking water is brought in and passed around clockwise.

For a humbling experience, spill a little water on mother earth without drinking any yourself and pass the drinking vessel to the next person on your left. When the sweat is over, rinse with cold water to strengthen your heart and close your pores.

The sweat lodge is not a torture chamber or a macho thing. It is a spiritual encounter and a discovery of life—a rebirth. It's like being in the womb of mother earth. After the sacred sweat ceremony is over, you crawl out from the protection of mother earth to return to the real world. For some, that's the hard part.

A sweat lodge ceremony can help you feel like a new human being. As a place of renewal and purification it is considered to be our church.

The sweat lodge is also used to heal the sick. In that ceremony, sometimes 104 stones are used, and it can last for a full day or longer. Healing medicine and herbs are brought in along with eagle feathers, or whatever other effects the holy person uses in healing. A Holy Man then conducts the ceremony. The Creator gives each Holy Man different medicine. Each medicine works in it own way, but I have left sweat lodges because the medicine did not feel right to me. During any ceremony, not just a sweat lodge, always exercise your right to walk out for your own reasons. Usually before I walk into any ceremony in which I don't know the medicine person, I find it comforting and protective to carry sage which is a purifier and protector.

On the other hand, participants should sometimes stay out of a ceremony when it doesn't feel right. I'm my own worst example. I had been drinking one night before a sweat lodge ceremony and felt rotten the next morning. I thought the steam would help take away the effects of the alcohol. When the first round of the sweat began, I realized that it wasn't just a steam bath but a purification of negative spirits. My body started burning all over. I experienced the most painful and agonizing sweat of my life. I stayed in all four rounds. Each round seemed to get worse, but finally it was over and I felt relief. The grandfathers had taken pity on my pathetic body. We dumped ice cold water on our bodies and left, but it wasn't yet over for me. I felt a sharp pain in my head and felt blisters on my shoulders and upper back.

I then understood what the medicine people meant when they said drugs and alcohol don't mix with spirituality and our path with the Creator.

Many medicine people believe that our Native American brothers and sisters who are serving time in prison would benefit from the sacred sweat lodge ceremony. Many have never experienced its purifying effects. Archie (Fire) Lame Deer is among the Holy Men who strive very hard to get our sweat lodges accepted into correctional institutions in California and elsewhere.

In the fall of 1985, I helped in ceremonies conducted by John Funmaker at the Rehabilitation Center in Norco, California. John is a dedicated medicine person and Sun Dancer. I've noticed great changes in these prisoners. They seem to gain a new goal in life and a renewal of hope and respect for themselves after experiencing sweat lodge ceremonies.

I especially remember a young Apache man who never said

much to us or the other prisoners. As the ceremonies progressed, his spirit seemed to awaken and he began to open up to others. He was getting ready to be released from prison. After taking part in the weekly sweats, he was more ready for the outside world than ever before.

Many of the incarcerated Native Americans are there because of drugs and alcohol which cultivates negative spirits in otherwise gentle human beings.

The Eagle Lodge in Long Beach, California is an alcohol and drug rehabilitation center where John Funmaker serves as a spiritual counselor. The center combines Native American spiritual ways with modern psychology to treat the alcohol and drug problems of our people. This approach has proven more successful than conventional methods. Through spiritual help, the sweat lodge, and the sacred pipe, many of these patients have found a new path free of alcohol and drugs.

One cold evening at the Eagle Lodge during the Christmas season, a man came to the Christmas party without a coat. When John Funmaker asked the man why he wasn't wearing a coat, the man said he didn't own one. Without hesitation, John took off his own jacket and gave it to the man.

I could tell that the people enjoyed themselves as sober, clear-minded individuals at this lodge. Their addictions were left behind, replaced with clean spirits. The Christmas feast seemed a celebration of their life and sobriety.

MEDICINE BUNDLES

Medicine Bundles are among a Native American's most sacred and holy personal belongings. The bundles are possessed by individuals, families, and societies within the tribes. Sometimes the bundles belong to everyone in the tribe.

These bundles can contain sacred pipes, animal parts, herbs, fetishes, cloth, stones, or anything else that an owner deems a sacred object. Objects are found in medicine bundles that are a mystery to everyone but the owner. Sometimes the bundles will be opened and displayed to help in a buffalo hunt or other hunting venture, for the well-being of a tribe, or in other spiritual rituals. The artifacts are always returned to the tribal bundle, and cared for and carried by a designated medicine person or elder. Tribes protect their medicine bundles with their very lives. It is believed that if the tribe's bundle is lost, all will suffer.

A personal medicine bag differs from the sacred medicine bundle in that the bag will contain a few pieces of herbs, stones, and other small medicines favored by the owner. It is usually carried around the neck or tied to a shirt, a coup stick, or a shield (which often has a vision painted on it), or tied to other personal objects.

Different types of medicines such as feathers, beads, paint, and animal parts also were tied or hung from weapons such as rifles, lances and bows and war clubs. Horses were decorated with these bags.

Most people are very secretive about their personal medicine bags, don't want them to be touched, or to let others know what is in them. Some are not so particular. It's individual preferences.

I have three small medicine bags. One bag contains personal, everyday protection such as sage, sweet grass, cedar and tobacco. The second contains a variety of medicine that has been given to me by Native Americans from different tribes. The third is very sacred to me and its contents, private.

Recently a family called on me to do a pipe ceremony for their young daughter who was about to reach puberty. They gave me tobacco and I did the ceremony at their home. The family was Buddhist but a friend of the family, who is a Native American woman, suggested to them that I come and help with the daughter's passage by performing a pipe ceremony.

I asked the Native American woman to make a small medicine bag about the size of a grape. After the pipe ceremony, I placed the ashes from the sacred pipe into the bag which also contained a small nest of sage. Then the bag was sewn closed and given to the young woman. She already had a larger medicine bag that would be worn around her neck. She placed the smaller one in it. This larger bag would contain objects of her choosing. I told her that the bag was hers to do with as she pleased. I also gave her some bitterroot to help soothe sore throats for her larger medicine bag. It is common practice for Native Americans to carry this root, especially singers.

Just as some people carry pill boxes, some people place their heart medicine and other prescription drugs in their medicine bags.

VII

THE SACRED ANIMAL WORLD

▲

Native Americans have great respect for the wild animals with whom they hunted and shared the land. The Indians and the wild animals lived life fully to the last breath. When death came, it was accepted as a natural act.

Domesticated animals are sad to me because they never had the freedom to fly, roam or develop their senses to survive in the wild. Even a wild rabbit will fight a coyote, wolf or wild cat.

When a cow is killed for food in our slaughter houses, it screams for its life. Adrenaline and fear runs through its veins. That taste of its fear is left in our mouths and bodies. When a buffalo was pursued by a Native American, it wasn't afraid and would fight to kill to the end.

The Native American imitated and learned survival techniques from the winged, finned, and four-legged creatures. We therefore have respect for the animals we kill to eat, and say prayers of thanks to them for giving their lives so that we may live.

Hunting was not a sport for Native Americans. They believed that all animals have a spirit. If killed improperly without due respect, its spirit will be offended. A hunter who didn't follow the hunting ways may find his attempts to kill hindered. This, in turn, might affect the entire tribe.

In revering the animals we kill to sustain us, we also prevent greed and senseless killing. Killing for food is the natural way of life for the Native American as it maintains the food chain.

Everything is on the menu. Even in death, our bodies were traditionally left above the ground as food for other animals.

Non-Indians and Native Americans alike have lost their interconnectedness and obligation to other species. So the bonds to other creatures have deteriorated with nothing to take its place. It is a loss for all.

The reality is that those of us with a Native American heritage live in a different culture today. We can't hunt, fish, and live off the land as we once did. Our ties to the wild animals, therefore, are not as strong as they were in the past. All animals had a purpose, even the pet animals of Native Americans, such as dogs. Dogs, who were often part wolf, pulled tribal belongings in a travois and would alert the tribes to approaching enemies.

All life, including the animal, is sacred to us, but some are more important than others because of our dependency on them for survival. Yet, the Native American knew that the loss of a single species of butterflies could tip the ecological balance against man.

In the Native American tradition, it is not unusual for animals to speak with us. Many have told stories about how they have spoken with animals, birds, and insects. I believe that the communication between humans and those of the animal world is not of words, but is a spiritual bonding that will direct us to what that creature has to show us. Although an animal has never spoken to me, I do feel guided by them.

ANIMALS OF THE PLAINS

Buffalo or bison are the largest mammals in North America, weighing up to 2,200 pounds. Once numbering in the millions, they have became nearly extinct. They are slowly returning today because they are a protected animal and are found on preserves, ranches, and reservations. Native Americans still consider them sacred.

The Native American Plains Indian coexisted with the buffalo in a way that sustained them. The buffalo was at the center of their ecological environment since their lives depended on it.

They always gave thanks to the killed animal and to the Creator for funishing it. This is similar to the Jewish tradition of making food "Kosher." Animals used for food must be slaughtered as humanely as possible. Only then can the meat be blessed by their Holy Man, a rabbi, and considered Kosher. Other foods must also be prepared according to dietary laws as reminders that eating and drinking are part of the sanctity of life.

Edgar Cayce, the Sleeping Prophet, said that if we take an animal's life for food, we should savor and respect it by making a banquet from its flesh.

Since the buffalo was so difficult to kill with a lance or bow and arrow, the Native Americans devised a buffalo jump in which they would drive a stampeded herd over the cliff. The buffalo jump saved the lives of many hunters who went in search of provisions for their families and the tribe. The jump also provided the hides that were needed for warmth, food, and shelter from the cold, hard winters of the plains. Buffalo jumps could provide all the hides needed for their tepees.

Thomas E. Mails, in *The Mystic Warriors of the Plains*, lists the many uses of the buffalo.

Horns: Cups, powderhorn, spoons, ladels, headdress and toys.

Hair: Headdress, saddle pad filler, pillows, ropes, ornaments, halters.

Hide: Moccasin tops, cradles, winter robes, bedding, breechclouts, shirts, leggings, belts, dresses, pipe bags, pouches, paint bags, quivers, tepee covers, gun cases, lance covers, and dolls.

Rawhide: Containers, clothing, headdresses, food, medicine bags, shields, buckets, moccasin soles, rattles, drums, ropes, saddles, knife cases, boats, quirts (short whips), bullet pouches, belts.

Tail: Medicine switch (used in ceremony), fly brush, lodge exterior decorations and whips.

Skin of the hind leg: Moccasins or boots.

Meat: Food (every part eaten), pemmican (converted), hump ribs, jerky, inner parts eaten on spot.

Skull: Ceremonies, sun dance and prayer.

Brains: Hide preparation.

Muscles: Sinew, bows, thread, arrows, cinches and glue.

Bones: Knives, arrowheads (ribs), shovels, splints, winter sleds, arrow straighteners, saddle trees, war clubs, scrapers (ribs), quirts, awls, paint brushes (hip bones), and game dice.

Whole animal: Totem, clan symbol, white buffalo sacred, adult yellow rare-prized.

Buffalo chips: Fuel, signals, and ceremonial smoking.

Four-chambered stomach: First stomach contains medicine for frost bite and skin disease. The liner is a container for carrying and storing water. Cooking vessel.

Scrotum: Rattles.

Paunch: Lining used for buckets, cups, basins and dishes.

Bladder: Sinew pouches, quill pouches, and small medicine bags.

Beard: Ornamentation, apparel and weapons.

Tongue: Best part of meat to eat.

Bears were revered for their wisdom. Crees called the bear by such names as Short Tail, Crooked Tail, The Angry One, and Four-Legged Human.

The grizzly was honored for its great strength. The grizzly traveled through the land fearing neither man nor other beast. In most confrontations, man lost to the grizzly until the introduction of firearms. Even with guns, man did not always win. Still, the grizzly is listed by the government as an endangered species.

Native Americans still imitate the bear in ceremony, as it is considered good medicine. The fact that the bear was one of the few animals that could walk on its hind legs like a man added more mystique to the creature. Besides its strength and wisdom, its body provides medicines such as bear oil used in ointment to treat rheumatism, dyes, and laxatives. Bear claws and teeth, especially those of the grizzly, are highly prized as necklaces.

Some Native Americans today are trying to halt the practice of killing bears for its bladder and stomach for use as an aphrodisiac. Ground up deer antlers also were thought to be an aphrodisiac. Medical scientists refute the notion that any of these substances enhance sexual prowess to any degree except psychologically.

Beavers are natural dam makers. They have the spirit of hard work, conscientiousness and persistence. If a hole is knocked in its dam, they will instantly begin rebuilding it and won't quit until it is done.

The beaver builds its dam downstream from its lodge to provide the needed water level for its family. The beaver's dam also makes a playgound for aquatic animals to gather and frolic, as well as providing a drinking place for other animals of the forest.

Native Americans used the beaver hide for hats, capes and mittens. During the fur-trade era of the early 1800s, the beaver was hunted nearly to extinction. The change in style to silk hats saved the remaining beaver.

Otter, the beaver's aquatic, clownish neighbor, has the opposite characteristics of the beaver. It is always playing and making fun of hard work, but is also very agile and resourceful. The other pelt is a very prized fur by both Native Americans and non-Indians because of its softness and sleekness. It is frequently used to make our pipe bags which are decorated with quill work, beads, bells, tin cones and horse hair.

Deer not only provided needed food, but many of its parts are used in decoration. The white tail of the deer is used in a roach headdress with porcupine guard hairs. It is also used for noisemakers worn on the clothes of dancers. Deer hooves were used to make medicine rattles. Many tribes used deer and elk skin for both clothing and moccasins because of its softness and pliability.

Plains Indians didn't hunt the deer as much as woodland and coastal tribes since the buffalo provided their primary source of meat. The white-tailed deer was mostly found in the eastern part of the United States, and the Mule deer on the Plains.

I have seen deer on the reservation in Montana mingling with cattle and bullalo. They seem to live in harmony with themselves and the humans around them. There also seems to be an abundant supply of meat for the people.

Eagles are special to Native Americans because they take our prayers higher and closer to the Creator than any other creature. The eagle is also a mighty hunter with sharp eyes. Its feathers, bones, talons, and sometimes the entire body are used in many of our ceremonies.

The Thunderbird's spirit which serves as messenger between the Creator and man, is represented by the eagle. Although the bald eagle is now found mostly in Canada, the northern United States, and Florida, it is considered an endangered species. The golden eagle is widespread in the western United States.

Fish weren't prized by most Plains Indians because they didn't think catching them was worthy of a hunter. Yet, if a Plains tribe fell on hard times and families were starving, fish were eaten. Native Americans who lived by the sea, however, often depended on it as their source of food.

Hawks along with the owl and the eagle were honored for their courage and spirit. An Indian boy might be told by his father to watch the hawk and try to mimic its accuracy. Warrior shields and dance regalia were decorated with hawk parts and feathers. Various types of hawks are found throughout the United States, including Swainson's, Red-tailed, Ferruginous, and White-tailed. Hawks are not as numerous as they once were and the Hawaiian hawk is on the endangered species list.

Horses, introduced to the Native Americans by the Europeans, not only brought a swifter means of transportation but increased their possessions and wealth. Before the horse, the Indian's possessions were few and had to be transported by dog or tribal member. The horse also expanded the areas for hunting and war. The Native American today jokes that the horse was the white man's apology for whiskey. Plains Indians became one of the best light cavalry in the world because of their riding skills and attunement to animals.

Horses made the smaller tribes more powerful in war. The horse was often elaborately decorated and painted with war honors and coup marks (for successful actions such as killing an enemy). Some horses even had war bonnets. One noted warrior was called, "Young Man Afraid of His Horses." This meant that when his enemies saw his horse, they fled in fear because they knew the warrior was near. A warrior's best horse was often killed at his death to carry him into the Great Mystery.

Today's Native Americans are still outstanding horsemen and champion rodeo riders. Many different tribes have their own all-Indian rodeos, such as the Crow Fair in Montana.

Mountain Lions, or cougars, are used in Native American medicine and held special meaning because they were rarely seen. They are highly tuned hunters themselves. A warrior or medicine person wearing a mountain lion's hide in war or ceremony demonstrated the wearer's stealth and agility.

The mountain lion has a very quiet way about it unless it is communicating to another of its kind. When it screams, it sends chills through your whole body. Just the Eastern cougar is on the endangered species list, but others have disappeared from much of the United States and are only found in wilder areas.

Owls, to the Plains Cree, are messengers of death. A retired Assiniboine elder living in Southern California told me of a visit from an owl at his home in the city. He said one day he heard some pecking on his front door, and when he opened the door, there was an owl. He said he slammed the door and went to the phone to call his sister on the reservation in Montana. He asked her if everyone was okay. His sister told him that one of the family members was very sick and dying.

A Holy Man instructed me not to use the owl's feathers, or other parts, because it could hurt my medicine. Some Southwest tribes and others look at the owl from a different perspective and use the feathers in ceremony.

Ravens, like many birds, are considered to possess supernatural powers. Many Native Americans believe it can change itself into different forms such as the Thunderbird or other animals. The raven, along with the magpie and the chickadee, were also bestowed with great wisdom.

Native Americans trusted this wisdom because the raven was sometimes thought to talk to people and guide them through unfamiliar paths of life. It is also the wolf's helper because it helps it find food by circling overhead near wild game. The wolf, in turn, leaves scraps from its feed for the raven.

Weasels (ermine, ferret) were noted for their swiftness of movement. Some tribes wore weasel skins as a safeguard against illness. The foot of the weasel was sometimes used as a love charm and worn by a man desiring a certain woman. Native Americans didn't consider the weasel "sneaky" like the white man. Perhaps the non-Indian farmer disliked the weasel because it developed a reputation as a killer of poultry. In reality, the weasel is a killer of rodents and therefore useful to those cultivating the land.

Wolves have mainly been treated as enemies by non-Indians who have all but destroyed them. Non-Indian children learned from early childhood to fear and mistrust the wolf with such tales as "Little Red Riding Hood," "Three little Pigs," and werewolf tales of horror. When an animal is feared and misunderstood it is often hunted to near extinction.

To the Native American the wolf exemplified craft in war, and was not known for maliciously harming man. It was killed only for the Indian's survival. Its fur was used for warmth and decoration. The wolf's skin was also used in the buffalo hunt by an Indian who would disguise himself in the wolf hide and crawl among the buffalo for the kill. Wolf's oil was also used to treat swelling in joints caused by rheumatism. The red wolf is on the endangered species list, and people are working very hard to introduce it back into the wilds of the southern United States and Mexico.

KEEPING ANIMAL PARTS

Because we honor all creatures and attribute certain powers to them, Native Americans keep animal parts. They just seem to come to us. People give them to you, they're passed down from family, or you find them in obscure places.

For instance, I was given some elk's teeth. This happened one day when I was looking through a collection of rocks belonging to the deceased uncle of a friend. We came upon some elk's teeth. My friend who had inherited this rock collection had no idea where the teeth came from. As we searched further, it became evident from a few other artifacts that her uncle, a loner who had traveled throughout the back country of the United States and Canada, had made friends with several Indian tribes. No one in the family had known much about him, and the find shed new light on his life. The elk's teeth was a great gift for me and was added to my collection.

Sometimes certain animal parts are kept for personal and ceremonial reasons such as bear fingers, wolf claws, elk ivory, and eagle claws. It is believed that in keeping the animal part one will gain the strength and power of that animal.

When white men came to a Plains Cree hunting lodge, they would be startled to see the severed heads of the animals hanging in a nearby tree. Usually a medicine person had instructed the Indian to do this. Since it was sacred medicine to them, the hanging animal heads had a different meaning than the trophies displayed on walls by white hunters.

Plains Cree and other tribes use buffalo skulls and other animal parts in ceremony and offering in order to bring that spirit to the circle and to our prayers.

Feathers, especially of the eagle, can be used in dance ceremony, healing, and other medicine ways to help keep one's path free from negativity and sickness. Most Native Americans take offense when they see the spirit of the sacred eagle used as decoration on cowboy hats or hanging on rear-view mirrors.

Eagle feathers come to people who know how to use them in the spiritual way. One of my eagle feathers was given to me by a powwow dancer who had danced all over the plains, and is, therefore, very special to me.

Eagle feathers gain spiritual power when used in prayer and ceremony. I recently gave away a feather I had used in my pipe ceremony to a Native American woman because I felt she needed the strength it had acquired through prayers. I continue to give away feathers and whenever I find myself in need they seem to come to me. If a person gets feathers in a wrong way, we believe they will be eaten by bugs and taken back to nature. One may also get arrested because they didn't have the right to possess those sacred feathers. Native Americans, however, are guaranteed by Article I of the Constitution of the United States of America of the legal right to own and use eagle feathers and parts in a spiritual way.

Some Holy Men are so adept at using the eagle feather that they can make you feel an eagle's presence when they're conducting a ceremony. During a sweat lodge ceremony in Santa Barbara, California conducted by Archie Fire Lame Deer, a Lakota Holy Man, I felt the spirit of the eagle touch me with its wing as it flew in a circle in the lodge. That is good medicine.

When an eagle is taken apart in ceremony, every piece is saved. All parts—claws, wings, feathers, bones—have spirit in them.

NATURAL ORDER TO A NATIVE AMERICAN

Native Americans don't believe that any animal should be caged, not even for its safety. When an animal is taken for food, it is natural for its fur or hair to be used for clothing. In this way, its entire being is respected. Within the circle of life this is the natural order; each animal is prey to another.

We also do not like to see wild animals raised in captivity for their furs. To me, that is like raising cattle who have never had any freedom. Native Americans used fur pelts for centuries. It helped keep them alive during cold winters. But the animals were free until death, as were Native Americans who were also subject to prey by the animals. When we offend this circle, the outcome sometimes teaches us a lesson.

Larry, a Native American friend, was reminded of this natural order of the circle when he saved a chipmunk from a hawk that was circling over it. He brought it home with him and made a home for it from an old bird cage. He fed and cared for it like one of the family.

The chipmunk got so fat that its neck and cheeks nearly rolled up around its head. Several times while Larry was feeding the chipmunk it lunged and bit him. Larry decided to take the chipmunk back to the area were it was found. He located a spot in the forest where a hawk again was circling overhead.

VIII

WAYS TO HELP HEAL GRANDMOTHER EARTH

▲

My belief is that the earth cannot be healed by technology alone. We need a change in values, and a reawakening of spirituality that leads to nurturing ourselves and the earth. We can no longer assume that life exists only for man's consumption. Our lifestyles may have to become less comfortable in order to revitalize grandmother earth.

We can educate ourselves on the environment, but we don't need to dissect the mystery of life. I believe in maintaining the mystery and awe to enhance our path. Albert Einstein said: "The most beautiful thing we can experience is the mysterious. It is the source of true art and science."

The following are ways to help heal the earth. They are based on the Native American tradition and involve not only the mysteries of life, but personal growth.

▲ Take time to turn over a rock and look at the world under it. Then put it back as it was.

▲ Learn to savor and enjoy the different seasons, and climatic changes.

▲ Celebrate life at every opportunity.

▲ Welcome the unknown, and wrap it around your body like a new blanket.

▲ Laugh at yourself when everything is bad. Look to the good.

▲ If you have a choice between laughing or crying, try to laugh, but crying is natural and healthy.

▲ If you build a house in the mountains, don't tear down the mountain.

▲ When using water use each drop wisely as if you were out in the desert with a limited amount.

▲ Use only what you need to sustain your household circle.

▲ Give thanks for the food that is available.

▲ Hunt only what is necessary for food. Kill animals only for eating.

▲ Don't kill predatory animals such as snakes. Learn to live in harmony with bugs and spiders.

▲ Respect those on other paths.

▲ Eat healthy, life-giving foods.

▲ Help people who are in need.

▲ Support causes that help save the earth.

▲ Savor each day by living one day at a time.

▲ Use positive action rather than negative thought.

▲ Cultivate a spiritual garden as you would a vegetable garden with effort and care.

▲ Feel nature's spirit when in the out-of-doors.

▲ Listen for the sounds of the animals.

▲ Travel light.

BIBLIOGRAPHY

▲

Brown, Joseph Epes. *The Spiritual Legacy of the American Indian*. New York: Crossroad Publishing Co., 1982.

Capra, Fritjof. *The Turning Point*. New York: Simon and Schuster, 1982.

Fine Day. *My Cree People*. Invermere, B.C.: Good Medicine Books, 1973.

Furst, Peter T. *Hallucinogens and Culture*. Novato, CA: Chandler & Sharp Publishers Inc., 1976.

Gibson, Arrell Morgan. *The American Indian*. D.C. Heath and Co., 1969.

Hail, Barbara A. *Hau, Kola!* Seattle, WA: University of Washington Press, 1983, third printing.

Hassrick, Royal B. *The George Catlin Book of American Indians*. New York: Promontory Press, 1981.

John (Fire) Lame Deer and Richard Erdoes. *Lame Deer Seeker of Visions*. New York: Pocket Books, 1972.

Lowie, Robert H. *Indians of the Plains*. Lincoln, NE: University of Nebraska Press, 1984.

Mails, Thomas E. *The Mystic Warriors of the Plains*. New York: Doubleday & Co. Inc., 1972.

National Geographic Society, editors of. *The World of the American Indian*. Washington, D.C.: National Geographic Society, 1974.

Vogel, Virgil J. *Amercian Indian Medicine*. Norman, OK: University of Oklahoma Press, 5th edition, 1982.

Weiner, Michael A. *Earth Medicine Earth Food*. New York: Collier Books. A Division of Macmillan Publishing Co. Inc., 1980.

Zotigh, Dennis. *Moving History: Evolution of the Powwow*. Edited by C.B. Clark, Ph.D.; Howard Meredith, Ph.D.; and Scott Tigert, M.A. Oklahoma City: The Center of the American Indian.

HERB RESOURCES

▲

Encyclopedia of Herbs. Emmaus, PA: Rodale Books, 1987.

Hutchens, Alma R. *Indian Herbology of North America.* Windsor 14, Ontario, Canada: Merco, 1973.

Kloss, Jethro. *Back to Eden.* Santa Barbara: Woodbridge Press Publishing Co., 1975.

Lust, John. *The Herb Book.* Simi Valley, CA: Benedict Lust Publications, 1974.

Ross, Jeanne. *Herbal Body Book.* New York: Grosset & Dunlap Publishers, 1976.

Santillo, Humbart. *Natural Healing With Herbs.* Prescott Valley, AZ: Hohm Press, 1984.

Tierra, Michael. *The Way of Herbs.* New York: Washington Square Press, 1983.

For more information contact: American Indian Herb Co., P.O. Box 16684, San Diego, CA 92116.

ANNUAL POWWOW EVENTS

▲

▲ All-Indian Rodeo/Parade, Klamath Falls, Oregon; May.

▲ All-Indian Powwow, Flagstaff, Arizona; July.

▲ American Indian Ceremonial Dancing, Taos, New Mexico; September.

▲ American Indian Corn Planting Ceremony, Allentown, Pennsylvania; May.

▲ Black Hills Stock Show and Rodeo, Rapid City, South Dakota; January.

▲ Buffalo Dance, Santa Clara Pueblo, New Mexico; June.

▲ Ceremonial Dances at Most New Mexico Pueblos; end of December.

▲ Cherokee National Holiday, Tahlequah, Oklahoma; August.

▲ Corn Dance, San Felipe Pueblo, New Mexico; May.

▲ Corn Dances, Cochiti, Santa Cruz and Taos Pueblos, New Mexico; May.

▲ Corn Dance, Santa Clara Pueblo, New Mexico; August.

▲ Corn Dance, San Ildefonsa Pueblo, New Mexico; September.

▲ Feast of the Flowering Moon, Chillicothe, Ohio; May.

▲ Grand Village of the Natchez Indian Fort, Natchez, Mississippi; September.

▲ Harvest and Social Dances, Laguna Pueblo, New Mexico; August.

▲ Harvest Dance, Isleta Pueblo, New Mexico; September.

▲ Hopi Snake Dance, Hotevilla and Shangopavi, Hopi Reservation, Arizona; August.

▲ Hopi Basket Dance, Hopi Reservation, Arizona; mid-October.

▲ Intertribal Indian Ceremonial, Gallup, New Mexico; August.

▲ Iroquois Indian Fest, Schoharie, New York; August.

▲ Mountain Eagle Indian Fest, Hunter, New York; August.

▲ Nanticoke Indian Powwow, Millsboro, Delaware; September.

▲ North American Indian Days, Browning, Montana; July.

▲ Old Pecos Bulls Dance, Jemez Pueblo, New Mexico; August.

▲ Poarch Creek Indian Thanksgiving Day Powwow, Atmore, Alabama; November.

▲ Powwow, Window Rock, Arizona; July.

▲ Rain Dance, Zuni Pueblo, New Mexico; June.

▲ Red Earth Celebration of the Indian, Oklahoma City, Oklahoma; June.

▲ Six Nations Native Pageant, Ohsweken, Ontario, Canada; August.

▲ Southern Ute Bear Dance, Ignacio, Colorado; late May.

▲ Turtle Dance, San Juan Pueblo, New Mexico; end of December.

▲ Ute Mountain Sun Dance, Towaoc, Colorado; July or August.

▲ Ute Mountain Bear Dance, Towaoc, Colorado; held in May or June.

▲ Yukon Indian Days, Teslin Lake, Yukon, Canada; July.

▲ Zuni Shalako Dance, Pueblo, New Mexico; early December.

▲   ▲   ▲

Many other powwows take place throughout the country other than the ones listed. For further information contact the city's chamber of commerce or travel information agency.

Arizona: Phoenix and Valley of the Sun Visitor and Convention Bureau, (602) 254-6500.

California: Chamber of Commerce: 1027 10th, Sacramento, California 95814. Toll-free travel information, 1-800-862-2543, xT100.

Colorado: Toll-free travel information, 1-800-433-2656.

Delaware: Chamber of Commerce, One Commerce Center, Wilmington, Delaware 19801. Toll-free travel information, 1-800-441-8846.

Mississippi: Chamber of Commerce, P.O. Box 1849, Jackson, Mississippi 39205. Toll-free travel information, 1-800-962-2346 or 1-800-647-2290 for out-of-state.

Montana: Chamber of Commerce: 2030 11th Ave., P.O. Box 1730, Helena, Montana 59624. Toll-free travel information, 1-800-541-1447.

New Mexico: New Mexico Travel Division, Joseph M. Montoya Bldg., 1100 St. Francis Dr., Sante Fe, New Mexico 87503. Toll-free travel information, 1-800-545-2040.

New York: New York State Department of Economic Development, 1 Commerce Plaza, Albany, New York 12245. Toll-free travel information, 1-800-225-5697.

Ohio: Chamber of Commerce, 35 E. Gay St., Columbus, Ohio 43215. Toll-free travel information, 1-800-282-5397.

Oklahoma: Oklahoma Tourism Department, P.O. Box 60000, Oklahoma City, OK 73146. 1-800-652-6552.

Oregon: Economic Development Department, 775 Summer St. NE, Salem, Oregon 97310. Toll-free travel information, 1-800-543-8838 or 1-800-547-7842 for out-of-state.

Pennsylvania: Chamber of Commerce, 222 N. 3rd St., Harrisburg, Pennsylvania 17101. Toll-free travel information, 1-800-847-4872.

South Dakota: South Dakota Tourism, 711 Wells Ave., Pierre, South Dakota 57501-3335. Toll-free travel information, 1-800-952-2217 or 1-800-843-1930 for out-of-state.

GLOSSARY OF
COMMON CREE WORDS

▲

HUMANS

Baby	Os-kah-wah-sis
Boy	Nah-pe-sis
A Cree	Ne-i-yahw
Child	Ah-wah-sis
Old Person	Ke-te-ah-yah
Man	Nah-pew
People	Ah-yi-si-yi-niw
White Man	Wah-pis-ki-wi-yahs
French Man	Me-mis-ti-ko-siw

ACTIONS

Cry	Mah-to
Eat	Mi-chi-so
Laugh	Pah-pi
Play	Me-tah-we
Sing	Ni-kah-mo
Work	Ah-tos-ke

RESPONSES

Yes	E-ah
Bad	Mah-yi
Good	Mi-yo
Right	Kwah-yahsk
Wrong	Nahs-pahch
No	Nah-mo-yah

CREE WORDS FOR COLORS

Red	E-mi-kwahk
Blue	E-ahs-ki-tah-kwahk
Green	E-os-kahs-ko-si-wahk
White	E-wah-pis-kahk
Yellow	E-o-sah-wahk
Orange	E-pah-kahs-ko-sah-wahk
Pink	E-o-ki-niw-wah-pi-kwah-ni-yahk
Purple	E-ahs-ki-tah-ko-pe-tik
Wine	E-wah-tow-ki-mi-kwahk
Brown	E-wi-pahk
Black	E-kahs-ki-te-wahk

CREE PLANT NAMES

Birch	Wahs-kwe-yah-tik
Blueberries	I-yi-ni-mi-nah
Chokecherries	Tah-kwah-i-mi-nah-nah

Cranberries	Wi-sah-ki-mi-nah
Gooseberries	Sah-sah-po-mi-nahk
Juneberries	Mi-ni-sah
Plums	Pah-ke-sah-ni-mi-nahk
Pine	Mi-nah-ik
Raspberries	Ah-yos-kah-nahk
Red Willow	Mi-kwah-pe-mah-kwah-tik
Trees	Mis-ti-kwahk
Willows	Ni-pi-si-vah

CREE NAMES FOR FOODS

Bread	Pah-kwe-si-kahn
Lard	Pi-miy
Maple Sugar	Si-si-pahs-kwaht
Meat	Wi-yahs
Milk	To-to-sah-poy
Pepper	Pah-pes-ko-min
Potatoes	Kis-ti-kah-nah
Salt	Si-wi-tah-kahn
Sugar	Si-wi-ni-kahn

CREE NAMES FOR ANIMALS

Animals	Pe-yahk pi-sis-kiw
Bat	Ah-pah-kwah-nah-chis
Bear	Pe-yahk wah-kah-yos
Beaver	Ah-misk
Bee	Ah-mo

Bird	Pe-ve-sis
Blackbird	Chah-chah-kah-yow
Bug	Mah-ni-chos
Butterfly	Kah-mah-mah-kos
Cow	Pe-yahk mos-tos
Coyote	Mes-chah-chah-kahn
Crow	Ah-ah-siw
Deer	O-kwah-kwe-pah-i-os
Dog	Pe-yahk ah-tim
Duck	Si-sip
Fish	Ki-no-sew
Fly	O-chew
Fox	Mah-ke-sis
Frog	Ah-yi-kis
Goose	Nis-kah
Hawk	Ke-kek
Horse	Pe-yahk mi-sah-tim
Lizard	O-si-ki-yahs
Mink	Sah-kwes
Moose	Pe-yahk mo-swah
Mouse	Pe-yahk wah-pah-ko-sis
Muskrat	Wah-chahsk
Owl	O-ow
Pig	Pe-yahk ko-kos
Rabbit	Wah-pos
Raven	Kah-kah-kiw
Skunk	Pe-yahk si-kahk
Snake	Ki-ne-pik
Squirrel	Ahn-kwah-chahs
Weasel	Si-kos
Wolf	Mah-i-kahn

CREE WORDS FOR EVERYDAY THINGS

Bed	Ni-pe-win
Blankets	Ah-ko-pah
Book	Mah-si-nah-kahn
Coat	Mis-ko-tah-kahy
Hat	Ahs-to-tin
Head	Mis-ti-kwahn
House	Wahs-kah-i-kahn
Medicine	Mahs-ki-ki-yah
Mouth	Mi-ton
Nose	Mi-kot
Pants	Mi-tahs
Robe (Covering)	We-we-kah-pi-win
Shoes	Mah-ki-si-nah
Story (Legend)	Ah-tah-yo-ke-win
Fur	Mi-kwah-tik
Wagon	O-tah-pah-nahsk

NUMBERS IN CREE LANGUAGE

One	Pe-yahk
Two	Ni-so
Three	Nis-to
Four	Ne-o
Five	Ni-yah-nahn
Six	Ni-ko-twah-sik
Seven	Te-pah-kop
Eight	E-yi-nah-new
Nine	Ke-kah-mi-tah-taht
Ten	Mi-tah-taht

CREE WORDS FOR THE OUTDOORS

Autumn	Tah-kwah-kin
Campfire	Ko-tah-wahn
Clouds	Wahs-ko
Creek	Si-pi-sis
Day	Ki-si-kahw
Daylight	Wah-pahn
Eclipse	Ko-tah-wiw-pi-sim
Lake	Sah-kah-i-kahn
Moon	Ti-pis-kahw-pi-sim
Morning	Ki-ki-se-pah
Night	Ti-pis-kahw
Rain	Ki-mo-wahn
Red Willow	Mi-kwah-pe-mah-kwah-tik
River	Si-piy
Road	Mes-kah-nahw
Sky	Ki-sik
Spring	Mi-vos-kah-min
Stars	Ah-cho-ko-sahk
Swampy Area	Mahs-kik
Summer	Ni-pin
Sun	Ki-si-kahw-pi-sim
Sunrise	Sah-kah-tew
Sunset	Pah-ki-si-mon
Today	Ah-noch
Tomorrow	Wah-pah-ki
Thunder	Pi-ye-si-wahk
Wind	Yo-tin
Winter	Pi-pon
Woods	Sah-kahw